Dear Reader,

Welcome back to Lancaster, Maine! The latest in the Tearoom Mysteries series promises plenty of intrigue for Jan, Elaine, and you, accompanied by lots of delicious tea and a new recipe for you to try out in your own kitchen.

Late summer in Lancaster is characterized by the last of the season's long, warm days, a special exhibit at the local art gallery, and an upcoming clambake. Though I make my home in the south, I've visited Maine and other parts of New England multiple times, and I love it more and more each time I go back, so writing this book was like getting to visit once again. There's something special about those little beach towns, where the locals welcome this visitor as if I were one of their own, and they're always happy to see me enjoy yet another slice of incredible Maine blueberry pie. And, of course, who can resist a clambake?

Unlike my relaxing Maine vacations, Jan and Elaine have plenty of hurdles to jump before they reach their own celebratory clambake, including a missing teddy bear and the sweet little girl he belongs to, but with God on their side and the help of their friends, they'll be well on their way to a happy ending to the summer season. I hope you'll enjoy their journey as much as I enjoyed creating it.

And may your own summers be filled with warmth and wonder.

Blessings,
Amy Woods

Tearoom Mysteries

Tearoom for Two
Tea Rose
To a Tea
Crosswords and Chamomile
Burning Secrets
O Christmas Tea
On Thin Ice
Tea Is for Treasure
Trouble Brewing
Mystery and Macarons
The Tea Will Tell
Tea and Touchdowns
Steeped in Secrets
Stealing Santa
A Monumental Mystery
Whispers from the Past
Tearoom in a Tempest
Brimming with Questions
Beneath the Surface
Apart at the Seams

TEAROOM
mysteries

Apart at the Seams

AMY WOODS

Guideposts

New York

Published by Guideposts Books & Inspirational Media
110 William Street
New York, New York 10038
Guideposts.org

Acknowledgments

Every attempt has been made to credit the sources of copyrighted material used
in this book. If any such acknowledgment has been inadvertently omitted or
miscredited, receipt of such information would be appreciated.

Scripture references are from the following sources: *The Holy Bible*, King James
Version (KJV). *The Holy Bible, New International Version*. Copyright ©1973, 1978,
1984, 2011 by Biblica, Inc. Used by permission of Zondervan. All rights reserved
worldwide. www.zondervan.com

Cover and interior design by Müllerhaus
Cover illustration by Ross Jones, represented by Deborah Wolfe, Ltd.
Typeset by Aptara, Inc.

Printed and bound in the United States of America
10 9 8 7 6 5 4 3 2 1

Apart at the Seams

CHAPTER ONE

These displays could rival a Smithsonian exhibit!" Elaine Cook exclaimed to her cousin, Jan Blake, as they toured slowly around the local art gallery in the small town of Lancaster, Maine. The Lancaster Veterans of Foreign Wars chapter had teamed up with sisters Rachel and Elsa Leon, who owned and managed Whisper Art Gallery, to put on a week-long event showcasing Heroes of Foreign Wars, and if the rest of the week continued as that Saturday morning, the exhibit promised to be a roaring success.

"It's wonderful to see these lives remembered," Jan said to her cousin. "The families kept so many mementoes of their loved ones who went off to serve overseas."

Elaine looked at her cousin, whose short hair featured only a hint of gray, like her own. Jan's blue eyes surveyed the large, open room in reverence. What Jan had observed was true. As they made their way around the gallery, Elaine saw photographs from Vietnam all the way through Iraq, articles of clothing worn by soldiers, newspaper clippings dating back to the 1940s, and tiny keepsake items such as jewelry, pins, and buttons. There was even a small shabby teddy bear, she noticed, perched atop a tattered green uniform jacket on one of the tables. Her heart melted at the images the bear brought to mind—had a child sent the stuffed animal with her father as a token when he went off to war? Or had a battle-weary papa brought it home with him to a wife or a waiting little one? Each proudly displayed piece held a heart's worth of memories, including Ben's camera, which Elaine had thought to add to a small display of Ben's belongings.

Her late husband, who had been a lieutenant colonel in the US Army, had served all over the world, and photography had been a hobby of his. The camera, she'd noticed that morning, still held a full roll of film—the little ticker showed zero photos had been taken, and she smiled sadly to think of Ben loading the roll hopefully. It had been a while since his passing, and she'd even been blessed to fall in love a second time, but she knew now that she would continue to miss him every day.

The townspeople had been invited to contribute any relics related to overseas wars in which American soldiers had served, and boy, had they come through in abundance. Besides the displays, the Leon sisters had hung black-and-white photographs along the walls where they usually displayed the work of local artists, and American flags in various sizes adorned the rafters.

"Well," Jan said, taking one last look around before glancing at her wristwatch, "I think our short break is up. We'd better get back to our table."

Elaine nodded and she and Jan made their way to the table they'd set up near the front by the gallery doorway. As co-owners of Tea for Two, a tearoom they'd opened together a few years back in the large lakeside Victorian they also shared as a home, the cousins had volunteered to cater this exhibit free of charge. As their business had become more and more popular and enjoyed growing success, Jan and Elaine did what they could to give back to their small, close-knit community.

As they drew near the table, Elaine admired the blue-and-white tablecloth Jan had chosen, and the red tea service she herself had picked out. Spread across the patterned fabric were miniature cupcakes with white frosting and tiny red and blue sugar sprinkles, alongside Jan's locally famous mini maple croissants and a tiered stand holding expertly sliced fruit.

A steady stream of visitors passed their table, and Elaine and Jan served tea and made sure there were plenty of treats available, restocking from the supply they'd brought anytime things got a little low.

Elaine was pleased to see many of their friends from Lancaster stop by, like Shane and Azalea Atherton, a young couple who worked helping Shane's mother, Macy, run Green Glade Cottages. They paused briefly at the tea table to say hello. With the line for the refreshments moving along at a brisk pace, all Elaine had time for was a quick greeting, after which she noticed Zale had on a beautiful, delicate gold bracelet when the young woman reached for a cupcake. Elaine complimented the pretty piece of jewelry and Zale, blushing a bit, said thank you before the couple moved forward to allow fellow locals Ryan and Felicia Standish to grab some goodies. The day and the small talk flew by, and before she knew it the crowd thinned. Glancing at her watch, Elaine noticed it was almost time for the exhibit to shut down.

As the last few visitors trailed out, Elaine and Jan said goodbye to Cora Packard, a navy veteran and the VFW's chapter representative, as well as to the other chapter members that had come to help sign in visitors and answer questions that day.

"We couldn't be happier with how well opening day turned out," Cora said as she lingered at their table. Tall and trim in her uniform, with intelligent gray eyes and a presence that was kind but commanding, the fifty-something veteran made it easy to guess she held her own in a predominantly male profession. "I think this event will go a long way toward sponsoring the handicapped-accessible van we're hoping to purchase."

"We're so glad to help out," Jan said, shaking Cora's outstretched hand. "It's the least we can do to thank you for your service."

With the gallery nearly empty, they packed up Elaine's car with their supplies and the remaining food before heading over to touch base with Rachel and Elsa, who were busy tidying up.

Rachel smiled as Jan and Elaine approached, the corners of her eyes crinkling softly behind the lenses of her glasses. Her shoulder-length hair was pulled back into a ponytail, and she wore a white button-down top, a purple denim skirt, and brown leather sandals. Rachel's skin was tanned and her limbs toned from her work as a volunteer firefighter. Elaine guessed she was around forty or so, and she was a pleasant person to be around. She shared the loft apartment above the gallery with her sister, Elsa, whose paintings the gallery most prominently featured.

"What can we do to help?" Jan asked, rubbing her hands together. Elaine could see that both sisters were tired from running around all day, making sure that everyone's questions were answered and that things ran smoothly. The gallery did well on a regular basis, but it wasn't often as crowded as it had been with the special exhibit going on.

"I think that's it for today," Rachel said, holding out her palms.

"We're all pretty beat," Elsa added. She was the more confident of the two sisters, though both were smart, pretty, and kind, and they seemed happy with the lives they'd built and with each other's company. That day, Elsa had traded the flowy bohemian-style clothing she usually preferred for an outfit similar to Rachel's—a top and cardigan over a modest skirt. Elaine grinned to herself though, seeing that Elsa had still added a flower to the loose bun at the nape of her neck.

"Agreed," Rachel said. "I couldn't be more pleased at how the day turned out, and I think the VFW will be overjoyed at the generous donations we'll be able to pass on to them at the end of the week," she added, pointing to a jar sitting atop a nearby table. "But I think I could use a break."

"We'll all be glad for a day off tomorrow," Jan said. "But why don't Elaine and I come by tomorrow after church to debrief on today, and help you set up for Monday?"

Elaine nodded. "That'll give us a chance to review and be ready for next week. I know it probably won't be as busy during the week as on a Saturday, but both the *Penzance Courier* and the *Weekly Wave* ran advertisements about it, and Cora said the VFW office phone rang off its hook last week with interested folks wanting to come by and see the displays."

"I have no doubt we'll get that handicapped-accessible van," Jan noted, sounding pleased.

Elsa and Rachel smiled at each other before Elsa said, "Sounds like a good plan. And I have no doubt the visitors' generosity has much to do with the deliciousness of Jan's pastries."

Elaine turned to see her cousin's expression brighten as Jan thanked Elsa for the kind words. Elaine couldn't agree more. When they'd first opened the tearoom, Jan had been a bit shy and reserved, but now she beamed when someone complimented her baking, and she deserved every word of it.

"Save a seat for us at church if you would, and afterward you can come by to talk about how today went and if we need to change or add anything for next week," Rachel said.

"Sure will," Elaine responded. She and Jan waved to the Leons and walked out to her car. Even after owning it for a few years, Elaine still liked the bright-red Chevy Malibu. The color was so cheery it always made her smile.

Elaine let the late-day sun bathe her face as they walked into the parking lot. The weather was another reason to smile. Late August in Maine was one of her favorite times of the year. Often the weather began to cool by then, with highs in the lower seventies and lows near the fifties. It was comfortably warm during the day and the night air cooled things off so it rarely got too hot.

When they had climbed inside the car and buckled up, Jan said, "That was wonderful, wasn't it? Looking around at all those photographs…I don't often think much about all the sacrifice our soldiers make with the hope that those of us back home can live normal lives. I'm sure you do, though, because of Ben."

Elaine turned the ignition, enjoying the warmth of the car seats after they'd sat in the sun all day. Her late husband had traveled a great deal for the army and their family had never really put down roots. All the same, she had felt privileged to see so much of the world. "I did, a lot, when we were in active service. Now, I think more about how nice it is to stay in one place for a while, and how blessed and comfortable our lives are."

"I had no idea we had so many veterans in Lancaster," Jan said. "When Cora called and we agreed to provide refreshments, I was a little worried we'd made too much, but I counted only three cookies left over! We'll have to make more for next week. With Labor Day coming in a couple of weeks, there might be lots of family members visiting for the rest of the summer who'd want to stop by the gallery."

Elaine glanced over at her cousin as the short drive ended and she pulled into the driveway at Tea for Two. Jan was positively glowing. "You're right. I hope you don't mind the extra busy-ness," Elaine said, feeling a little guilty, as she was the one who'd said yes the instant she'd heard Cora's request, only running it by Jan afterward.

"Are you kidding?" Jan said, waving a hand to dismiss Elaine's concern. "I'm just happy to have new guinea pigs for my recipes. You keep me on my toes!"

Smiling, the cousins unloaded the trunk of the car and headed inside.

THE NEXT MORNING, Jan woke to strange silence. She usually woke with an alarm, and as she slowly opened her eyes, she realized it was far too bright in her room. She looked at her bedside clock and sat up with a start. She'd forgotten to set her alarm and slept late!

After rushing through her shower, she dressed quickly in a cheery yellow button-down shirt and a soft gray cotton skirt, stuffing her feet into sandals. She grabbed her Bible, cell phone, and purse and hurried down to the first floor, taking the stairs two at a time.

"Elaine!" she called out. "I'm sorry, but I slept in. We've got to run if we want to get into church before the sermon starts."

She made her way to the kitchen, fully expecting her cousin to be there waiting for her, having already read the paper and eaten breakfast, but Elaine was nowhere to be seen. Jan was just about to go back up to knock on her cousin's door when she heard footsteps rushing down the stairs.

Elaine burst into the kitchen. "Sorry I'm late," she said. "I slept in."

Jan couldn't help but laugh. "So did I! I thought I'd find you down here all ready to go, annoyed at having to wait for me," Jan said. "Need anything to munch on for the road?"

"Nah," Elaine answered, waving a hand as she opened the door. "I'll just eat when we get back."

Jan shrugged, deciding she wasn't too hungry herself. Her body hadn't quite figured out it was awake yet, so her stomach wasn't grumbling.

Once they'd gotten into Jan's old blue Camry, both women looked at each other and laughed again. "I can't believe we both goofed," Elaine said.

Jan shook her head and started the car before pulling out of the drive and onto Main Street. "I guess we were more tired than we thought. We were up extra early yesterday to start tea and pastries, and we didn't leave the gallery until after six, and the tearoom's been so busy lately with summer tourists that we haven't had a chance to really rest."

"Plus, we have the Labor Day clambake coming up in two weeks, and the planning has been busy."

Jan pulled off Pine Ridge Road into the Lancaster Community Church parking lot and found a spot. The cousins grabbed their purses and Bibles and went inside, quickly heading for a pew instead of stopping to chat as they normally would have.

"Remember, we've got to save seats for the Leons," Elaine reminded Jan.

"You don't think they're already here?" Jan whispered, trying not to draw too much attention as the notes of the first hymn began.

Elaine looked around at the mostly full pews and bit her lip. "I don't see them, do you?" she asked.

They settled into a half-empty row and Jan glanced around as well. "No, I don't."

The cousins looked at each other. "Maybe the same thing happened to them—they worked even harder than we did, setting everything up yesterday. Do you think they could have slept in too?" Elaine asked.

"It's certainly possible," Jan answered. "Elsa had already hung most of the photos and paintings by the time we got to the gallery yesterday morning. I know she was so proud and honored when Cora asked them to host the event, but I think perhaps it was a little busier than she thought it would be. The gallery's successful, but from what the sisters say, it's mostly a slow and steady stream of tourists—rarely a huge crowd like yesterday."

"*Hmm*," Elaine murmured. "Well, I don't see anybody else that needs a seat, so I'll leave my purse here next to me in case they come in late."

Jan nodded, reaching into the wooden pocket of the pew in front of her to grab a hymnal, and Elaine did the same. After the congregation finished the first song, there were a few moments to greet neighbors. Jan said hello to Ned and Rue Maxwell, asking after their daughter, Melissa, a geologist. When Rue patted Jan's hand and turned to catch up with Alan and Maureen Oakley, Jan took a moment to look around again, hoping to spot Rachel and Elsa. Sure, it was possible that the younger women had just been too tired to come, but Jan had a strange feeling about it that just wouldn't let up.

"Have you seen the Leons yet?" she asked Elaine, who'd just finished speaking to Bristol and Mark Payson in the pew in front of theirs.

"No," Elaine answered, turning to check behind Jan. "I'm sure they just decided not to come today."

Jan frowned. "You could be right, but then why would they specifically ask us to save them a seat?"

Elaine's brows knit. "Good question. It does seem odd."

"I'm worried about them. It's not like Rachel or Elsa to back out of something, and they both have our numbers. I'm sure they would have texted if they weren't going to make it," Jan said, the butterflies in her stomach fluttering faster.

Elaine put a hand on Jan's forearm. "If you feel that strongly, let's go over and check on them."

Jan hesitated a moment, then nodded.

The cousins slipped out of their pew and made their way outside the church to the car. As Jan drove past the marina and into view of the art gallery, she gave a little gasp. Police cars with flashing lights dotted the gallery's parking lot.

CHAPTER TWO

L ooks like your instinct was correct," Elaine said quietly. She turned to look at her cousin's pallid face. Elaine knew just how Jan felt. Her stomach turned as she thought of how she'd assured Jan in church that everything was okay and the Leons were fine. She was glad they'd followed Jan's hunch instead.

As soon as the car stopped, the cousins threw open the Camry doors and sprang from their seats.

"What happened, Dan?" Jan asked, jogging toward State Trooper Daniel Benson, her voice pitched high with worry. She and Elaine had helped the officer solve enough local mysteries that they were all on a first-name basis.

As Elaine caught up with Jan, Dan nodded to the officer with whom he'd been speaking and turned to answer Jan's question. "Looks like a break-in," he said. His blue eyes were serious in the morning sun as he leaned against his SUV. "How did you two hear about it?"

Elaine and Jan looked at each other.

"We didn't," Elaine said, her heart in her throat as she prayed silently that a break-in was all that had happened. "Rachel and Elsa Leon were supposed to sit with us at church this morning, but they didn't show."

"We were going to meet up at church and then all come back here to plan and set up for this week," Jan added, wringing her hands. Elaine put a hand on her cousin's shoulder to comfort her, knowing they were both hesitating to ask what had gone on inside the gallery.

"For the Heroes of Foreign Wars exhibit?" Dan asked, pulling his notebook and a pencil out of his pocket to jot down what they were telling him.

"That's right," Elaine said, nodding. "We provided the refreshments for opening day."

"Yesterday?" Dan asked.

"Yes, yesterday. Saturday," Jan clarified.

Dan stopped writing and put the pencil eraser against his chin, thinking. The sunshine bounced off his sandy hair. It was going to be a beautiful late-summer day, Elaine thought, and wondered if it would seem so to Rachel and Elsa.

"And neither of you have seen or spoken to either sister since?" Dan asked.

"No," Elaine and Jan said in unison.

"I just had a bad feeling in church when they didn't show," Jan added, then bit her lip. "Are they all right?"

Dan nodded. "A little shaken up, but not hurt."

The cousins shared a relieved glance, and Elaine said a silent prayer of thanks.

"Can we speak to them?" Jan asked nervously.

"I don't see a problem with that," Dan answered, his tone friendly and warm. "In fact, you might be able to get them to open up a little more."

Elaine knew that she and Jan occasionally exasperated him with their particular style of trying to help solve local crimes, but Dan, who had a wife and young children, was good-hearted and kind, and she knew that above all he appreciated their help, even if he did occasionally question their methods.

"Thank you, Dan," Elaine said, offering a warm smile.

The trooper nodded. "I'll follow you inside," he said, pointing his pencil toward the gallery building. "I know you know this, but I have to say it anyway—be careful not to touch anything. The tech is almost finished gathering prints and collecting evidence, but it's still an active crime scene. We can't risk any contamination."

"We understand," Jan said as the three of them walked toward the gallery.

The front entrance was wide open, but a quick check told Elaine there wasn't any broken glass, which meant either this wasn't the culprit's point of entry, or he or she had found a way to unlock the door. The cousins had barely stepped foot inside, Dan following behind, when Rachel and Elsa Leon rushed forward.

"Oh, we're so glad you're here!" Rachel exclaimed. "It's been a terrible night."

"So we've heard," Jan said gently.

Elaine studied Elsa and Rachel, who were in clear distress. The first thing she noticed was that Elsa was wearing a cotton pajama shirt and bottoms, her long hair hanging over her shoulder in a messy braid with strands sticking out all over. Rachel, too, wore pajamas. It must have been a long morning for the sisters.

"I know you've already talked to the police, but can you tell us what happened?" Elaine asked.

"Perhaps we should take care of first things first," Jan suggested. "Have you two had anything to eat or drink yet today?"

Elaine sent Jan a grateful look. She'd been so eager to dive in and start gathering information so she and Jan could help that she'd forgotten to start with the basics.

"Jan's right," she said, looking from Elsa to Rachel. "You would probably both feel better if you had a little breakfast."

Elsa grimaced. "I don't think I could eat a thing, but something hot to drink does sound good."

Rachel nodded. "Let's all go upstairs and I'll make us some coffee."

The cousins nodded in agreement.

"We'll go upstairs," Elaine said, "but Jan and I will make the coffee while you two sit down and take a break. Dan, is that all right?"

Dan glanced around the gallery and Elaine took a moment to do the same. The crime scene tech appeared to have finished his work and was busy scrolling through photos on his digital camera. It was strange, Elaine noticed—other than a few crooked pictures on the walls, there didn't seem to be a mess, at least that she could see.

"That'll be fine," he said, "on one condition."

"Let me guess," Jan said. "You'd like a cup of coffee too."

Dan grinned. "You know me too well."

Jan, Elaine, and Dan followed Rachel and Elsa upstairs to the apartment they shared above the gallery. It was small, with a bedroom and bath on either side of the living room and a kitchenette, but it was clean and tidy, and the sisters had decorated it with good taste and plenty of soft feminine accents. The result was cozy and inviting.

Elsa and Rachel led Dan to the living room, where he sat in a chair and the sisters took the couch. Jan and Elaine hurried to the kitchenette and quickly found coffee supplies and tea bags. In a matter of minutes, they'd finished brewing the hot beverages and brought everything out to the living room coffee table.

Once everyone had fixed their drinks the way they liked them, Elsa took a long sip, closing her eyes. "This coffee is excellent, thank you," she said.

"It's the least we can do," Elaine said. Jan had left the coffee to her, since she was more of a fan.

Elsa swallowed. "Well, it all started when I heard a loud crash, early this morning. I didn't check my bedside clock, but I think it must have been around three thirty or four."

The cousins nodded encouragement.

"Rachel heard it too," Elsa continued. "When I came out of my room, she was standing in the hallway, and we both heard another crash. Rachel was carrying the baseball bat she keeps under her bed, and I had my golf club."

Rachel took a sip of her coffee and nodded. "We were about to go downstairs to find out what was going on—we thought maybe a raccoon had gotten in or something—but then we heard an even louder sound." She took a deep breath.

"It sounded like a gunshot," Elsa said. "It scared us both, so we decided to stay up here and call the police."

"That's right," Rachel said. "And while we were waiting, I went over to the window to see if I could see anything. The lights from Main Street are pretty bright, but the parking lot was full of shadows."

"As she was looking out," Elsa said, gripping her mug, "I heard a vehicle peel out."

"Did you see it while you were looking out the window?" Jan asked.

"I didn't from my window," Rachel said, "but Elsa saw something when she looked out of the one on the other side of the apartment."

"I ran over when we heard the tires, but all I could confirm was that it was probably an SUV, and it seemed to be black or navy—a dark color that was hard to pinpoint in the night," Elsa said.

"Did you see the plates?" Elaine asked, leaning forward in anticipation.

Elsa shook her head. "Unfortunately, no, I couldn't discern any numbers or letters."

"But she did see that the plate wasn't from Maine," Dan said, "which could certainly prove to be helpful in narrowing it down. That is, once we process the other evidence."

Elaine's ears pricked up as she took a sip of the strong coffee she'd made. "What other evidence did you find?" she asked, meeting Jan's sharpened glance.

Rachel and Elsa shared a look. "When Dan investigated the gallery, he found out that we were right about the gunshot," Elsa said, her throat catching on the ominous word.

"No one was hurt?" Jan asked, the lines around her mouth deep with concern.

Both sisters shook their heads. "Thankfully, no," Rachel answered.

"The bullet appears to have gone through a wall in the gallery," Dan continued as he laid out the facts of the break-in. "And we didn't find any blood at all, which makes me think it was fired as a warning shot from one person to another. There had to have been more than one trespasser, because the sisters were quiet up here and didn't pose a threat to whoever broke in. Someone seems to have encountered someone else they considered a menace. We think it's possible that the person not driving the SUV got away on foot, since there were a few prints found outside—probably male, about a size eleven. That perp parked farther away, because the prints stopped near a separate set of tire tracks, which then drove off toward Main Street."

"Did you find the bullet?" Elaine asked.

"Sure did," Dan said, nodding before draining the last of his coffee. "From my experience, it looks a lot like the type used in a nine millimeter—likely a Glock 43 or something similar. Unfortunately, if that's the case, it's an extremely common handgun," Dan explained, seeing that Elaine appeared impressed that he could guess so quickly.

"We'll check the casing for fingerprints and have the lab run striation testing to see if we can confirm the type and model of firearm, but we won't be able to match it to the actual weapon since there was no gun left at the scene. Then, of course, we'll ask visitors about any SUVs and plates that might match the one Elsa saw."

"Does the gallery have security cameras?" Jan asked hopefully, but she was certain Dan would have already posed the question.

Rachel briefly squeezed her eyes shut and hung her head before looking back up to answer. "Yes, it does. However," she began, wringing her hands, "the cameras are currently at Computer Gal being fixed."

Elsa looked at her sister with sadness in her eyes. "There was a problem with the Bluetooth connection and they kept rebooting themselves over and over again. Diane said she figured out the problem and will be done working on the cameras soon, but Rach and I weren't too worried about it because our inventory has never held extreme value."

Rachel nodded. "The work we purchase is wonderful, and we take pride in our selection of art, but with the exception of a few larger pieces, the majority of our stock is priced so that people with any budget are able to buy and enjoy something. And the Heroes exhibit relics are of sentimental, not monetary, value," she explained.

"Plus," Elsa added, "we've lived here for years and have never had a break-in."

Rachel shook her head and opened wide her palms. "I can't imagine it would be worth the trouble."

"The proceeds from yesterday for the VFW are safe?" Elaine asked.

"I had the jar up here in my bedroom," Elsa said, "and the cash register in the gallery wasn't touched."

Everyone had finished their drinks, so Jan began clearing the coffee table. Elaine helped her bring the dishes back to the kitchenette, and together they loaded the dishwasher, added detergent, and set it to run.

"A gunshot going off in the art gallery is a big deal. I'm so thankful no one was hurt, but it won't take long for word to spread around town that someone broke in," Elaine said.

"Especially with this big exhibit going on." Jan pursed her lips.

"Let's make sure the Leons are going to be okay, and then we'll head back down to the gallery and take a look," Elaine suggested.

Jan nodded and they returned to the living room. Poor Elsa had red-rimmed eyes and Rachel was beginning to nod off.

"Why don't you two go back to bed?" Jan suggested, her tone soothing. "We've got the dishwasher going and there's no more to be done for now. We'll see Dan out while you both get some much-needed rest."

"That sounds like a fine idea," Dan said, standing. "Thank you for the coffee."

"Oh, don't thank us," Elsa said, stifling a yawn. "Elaine's coffee is way better than mine." She smiled softly and Elaine patted her arm.

"We'll be back tomorrow morning to set up for the day and to make sure you're doing all right," Jan promised. "Be sure to call us if you need anything."

Rachel nodded and stretched sleepily, looking as though she'd like to just curl up right there on the couch instead of making the long journey back to her bed. Jan, Elaine, and Dan said goodbye and started back down the stairs.

"I've got a locksmith coming to change the locks today—for the gallery doors and the Leons' apartment," Dan said quietly when they'd all reached the ground floor.

"Was there any other evidence besides the bullet hole, casing, and bullet? How about SUV tracks and footprints?" Elaine asked as Dan led the cousins through the gallery.

"As a matter of fact—yes there was," Dan said, stopping midstep. "And that's where things get really strange."

"What do you mean, *strange?*" Elaine asked.

Dan's eyes narrowed in thought. "I think it's best if you just see for yourself."

Jan and Elaine exchanged a look as they followed Dan further into the gallery. Finally, he stopped at a table and lifted up the cloth that covered it.

"Take a look," he said, waving a hand underneath the surface.

Jan and Elaine bent to peer into the shadowy space under the table.

"Oh my," Jan said, covering her mouth in surprise.

"That looks like quite a bit of money," Elaine said as she studied a navy-blue duffel bag, from which several large bills spilled. A few loose bills were strewn on the floor around the bag as well. From what she could see, it looked like several thousand dollars.

"Mmm-hmm," Dan agreed. "The question is, what kind of prowler breaks into a place and *leaves* money? In my experience, it's usually the other way around."

"Right," Elaine said. "And this is a small-town art gallery. The Leons wouldn't have had much cash around to steal anyway."

"So, whoever left this may have come for something other than cash," Jan said, placing a finger on her chin.

Dan raised his eyebrows. "The Leon sisters used their inventory list to check around and they didn't notice anything missing, but of course, hard to say for sure. Something could have slipped past the initial inventory." He looked at Elaine and then at Jan. "Would you mind walking through, since you were here during opening day? Everything's been dusted for prints already and the Leons are so tired after being up half the night and giving statements that I figure it would be helpful to have two more pairs of eyes."

"Happy to," Jan said, turning to Elaine. "Let's get to it then."

The cousins walked off in opposite directions, and Elaine passed by a few tables that looked as they had the day before. Then she came to the table that held Ben's camera. *Where is it?* she thought, her heartbeat thumping faster as she realized it might be missing. She began to walk away to let Jan know when her toe bumped into something. Bending, she saw Ben's camera lying on its side just under the table. She picked it up to examine it for damage, but everything looked fine. Turning it in her hands, though, she came across something different.

"Jan!" she called across the room.

Her cousin stopped midstep and hurried toward Elaine.

"What is it?" Jan asked, sounding worried.

Elaine held up the camera. It wasn't ancient—Ben had purchased it about twenty years before he died. But it was analog—a film camera, rather than a digital one—and of middle-range quality. It was a good camera—not the most expensive one he could have bought, but she recalled that her husband had spent a while saving up for it and loved using it.

"Look here," she said, pointing at the film ticker. "It's showing a two."

Jan squinted at the small number. "Sure is," she said. "How many did it have before?"

"Zero," Elaine said, unable to help the grin that ticked up the corners of her mouth. "These could be from the crime."

Jan frowned. "You think someone took pictures during the break-in?"

"Well, no," Elaine mused. "That would be strange, wouldn't it? I'm guessing it got knocked over and that somehow pushed the shutter button. But who knows? Maybe someone did intentionally take the pictures. Maybe the person who got shot at grabbed it as a last-ditch effort to identify the shooter."

"Definitely possible," Jan agreed. "The only thing to do is to get the film developed and find out." She paused, as something seemed to occur to her. "Are you absolutely certain there weren't any pictures on there before?"

Elaine nodded. "One hundred percent," she said firmly. She held up the camera. "I checked it over thoroughly, and the counter was at zero when I brought it in yesterday."

Jan nodded.

"I'll take this in to develop it as soon as I get a chance, but first I have to let Dan know," Elaine said.

The cousins found Dan chatting with a lab tech. Dan assured them that the camera had already been dusted for fingerprints, and Elaine was in the middle of telling him about the newly discovered photos when they saw a young woman pull up in an older-model sedan and hurry toward where they stood.

"Hi there," Dan said, reaching out a hand. "I'm State Trooper Daniel Benson."

The young woman tentatively accepted Dan's outstretched hand. She couldn't have yet reached thirty, Elaine thought, noticing her smooth forehead and no hint of crow's feet at the corners of her pretty brown eyes. Her ash-blonde hair was pulled back into a short ponytail, wispy bangs skimming her eyebrows. The little girl at her side—a daughter, Elaine assumed from the protective way the young woman held her hand—appeared to be about six or seven, with features favoring her mother's. The child smiled nervously and ducked behind her mother's leg when Elaine caught her eye.

"This is Elaine Cook and Jan Blake," Dan added, pointing at each cousin in turn. They nodded at the woman and offered her warm smiles.

"My name is Jessica Lachlan, and this is my daughter, Hattie," the woman offered.

Jessica's name sounded familiar and it only took a second for Elaine to place it. Not long ago, Pastor Mike had spoken to Elaine about her, and asked Elaine in confidence to befriend Jessica. She hadn't lived in town long and seemed lonely, he'd said, as if she'd come to Lancaster all on her own, with no family in the area. From what Mike had said, Jessica was quiet and kept mostly to herself, spending much of her time working hard or doting on her daughter. From all accounts, she was a good person and a caring mother. Elaine had wanted to reach out, but she had not yet seen Jessica around town. Elaine's heart went out to her now. How difficult it must be to have such a small child and not have anyone close by to help.

"Is there something I can do to help you?" Dan asked gently.

Jessica let go of Hattie's hand, the little girl clinging to her leg, and wrung her own together. "I'm glad to meet you all," she said sweetly. "It's about my daughter, actually."

"Is everything okay?" Dan asked, his voice firm and warm.

"Oh yes," Jessica said. "Hattie's fine. Except that, well, she seems to have left something here yesterday when we came to see the exhibit."

"You were here?" Elaine asked. "I'm so sorry I missed you. We were at the refreshments table all day and I didn't see you come through the line."

Jessica's cheeks turned a little rosy. "We had just eaten beforehand," she said. "You see, my uncle is in town and he's a veteran, so we stopped by, but we didn't stay long."

"How nice that you're getting to spend time with family," Jan said, smiling.

Jessica looked down at her feet. "Yes, it is nice." She paused. "Anyway, Hattie contributed her teddy bear here in one of the exhibits, but she was only going to leave him for opening day. He's very important to her—he's kind of a family treasure from my father who served in the Gulf War—and she didn't want to let him go for long. But I was distracted yesterday and had to get to work soon after, so we forgot to take the bear home with us."

"I'm sure that won't be a problem," Elaine said, catching Dan's eye to see if removing the bear would disturb the crime scene. Surely not—it was only a little girl's teddy bear. What harm could it do to allow her to take him home with her?

Dan nodded.

"I think I remember where he was," Jessica said.

"Take your time, but please don't touch anything other than the bear," Dan said, watching carefully as the woman and her daughter wandered toward the back of the gallery.

"You're not worried about the crime scene, Dan?" Jan asked.

He shook his head. "No. It's already been processed and I've given the Leons permission to clear up. We've taken photos of everything."

"Poor darling," Elaine said, watching after the little one as she hurried along behind her mother.

While they were gone, Elaine explained to Dan about the camera, promising to give him copies if the film turned up any genuine photos. Jan listened intently.

"If there are any actual photographs, and it's not just blanks, then it's important for you to get copies to me right away. If there are legitimate photos, then once we get those, I can have our guy at the office increase the size and zoom in so we can look for details," Dan said.

Elaine fully intended to ask him for copies of the enhanced images. She felt terrible for Rachel and Elsa. A break-in was one thing in their small town—awful, yes, but not the end of the world—but the gunshot? That meant a possibly dangerous person was running around town with a loaded weapon, and had threatened their friends. Who else might he threaten? Would he harm anyone? Elaine didn't know, but she intended to help Dan find out, and she knew Jan would too.

"That sounds good," she said to Dan, who was carefully watching Jessica and Hattie. "I'll call you as soon as I have them."

Elaine was just about to ask Jan if she was ready to go when she heard a little cry that caused her to look up sharply just as Jessica and Hattie came running over to where they stood.

"What is it?" Jan asked.

Jessica's features showed sadness and distress, but it was the look on the little girl's face that broke Elaine's heart.

"It's my bear!" Hattie cried out, her voice shrill and worried. "He's gone!"

Jan turned to Dan. "I thought nothing had gone missing," she questioned.

Dan frowned and scratched his chin in confusion. "So did we," he said, looking down as Hattie's nose scrunched up and a single tear slid down one little pink cheek. "Until now."

CHAPTER THREE

Jan's heart ached as she watched Hattie try to explain where she'd last seen her teddy bear the day before. Finally, as her daughter became more and more anxious, Jessica stepped in and spoke to Dan.

"It was at that table near the back," she said, pointing. "We even took a picture of the bear." She pulled a cell phone out of her pocket and showed it to Dan, Jan, and Elaine.

Sure enough, there sat the little guy atop a table covered in small memorabilia. The group walked over toward the very same table, and Jan instantly saw that everything was as it had been—except, of course, for the bear.

Dan studied the picture carefully for a moment, as if memorizing it. "I'll need you to email me this photo, if you don't mind. Can you think of anything else I should know about the bear? Anything special or out of the ordinary?"

To Jan, it looked completely ordinary—brown, worn, and fuzzy, with no plastic eyes or any limbs missing. It could have been any teddy bear. Its most remarkable qualities, if they could be called that, were that it looked to be quite old, shabby, and well loved.

"No, not at all," Jessica began, squeezing little Hattie's hand before pulling a tissue out of the small purse at her side. "That is, not to anyone else. It had sentimental value to my daughter, as you can see, and to me as well. My father gave it to my mother before he died in the Gulf War, and she gave it to me. It was always there, from as early as I can recall, and then I handed it down to Hattie when she was a baby. It's sort of a family heirloom, but it has no worth at all other than sentimental."

"He's my best friend," Hattie said.

The child was crying quietly rather than throwing a fit, and Jan's heart swelled even more. "We'll do the best we can to find him for you, okay?" she said, placing a hand on the little girl's shoulder.

Hattie looked up. "You will?" she asked softly, her voice sounding a little stronger.

Jan saw the warning look on Elaine's face, and she knew it was risky to make a promise to the child, but she couldn't help herself. "Absolutely," she said. "And my cousin will help. Won't you, Elaine?" Jan asked.

Elaine nodded, smiling sadly. "Of course I will."

Dan looked between the cousins, his expression a reflection of the look Elaine had worn a few seconds before. He turned to Jessica. "You're certain it's not valuable?"

She nodded.

"Do you know the brand or where it's from?" Dan asked.

"I'm sorry, but no," Jessica told them. "It never had any tags that I knew of, though it's possible I tore them off as a child. And, other than what I've told you about how my father sent it to my mother from the war via my uncle, I don't know anything else about its origin."

"All right then," he concluded. "We'll have to find out why someone may have wanted to take the toy. In the meantime," he said, pulling a business card out of his pocket, "here's my info. Please call me if you think of anything else we might need to know. And e-mail me that picture as soon as you can."

Jessica agreed to do so and gave Dan her number as well. Taking Hattie's hand, she said goodbye to the three of them and headed back out to her sedan.

Dan watched as the little family of two pulled out of the gallery drive. "What on earth are we dealing with here?" he wondered aloud. "We've got an ordinary missing teddy bear, a bag full of money, and a bullet hole in the wall. And possibly the casing and the bullet itself."

"And don't forget some vague information about a possible SUV," Jan added. "Sure isn't much to go on."

"No, it's not," Dan agreed, rubbing the bridge of his nose. "Who in their right mind would steal a worthless stuffed animal and leave behind a bunch of money?" He raised his palms. "This is either the dumbest person—or people—I've ever come across, or they know something we don't. I'm going to need all the help I can get."

"I'm going to assume it's the latter," Jan said. "And you know we'll be glad to help, Dan. That's what we're here for."

THE NEXT MORNING, Monday, Jan got up early to do the baking for the breakfast crowd at Tea for Two, while Elaine drove over to the Leons' gallery to deliver the day's refreshments, help the sisters set up for the day, and see how they were faring after the break-in. Elsa and Rachel were still a little on edge, but they seemed far better, and definitely more rested, than they had on Sunday. Once she was sure everything would be fine without her there, Elaine started back to the tearoom.

She pulled off Main Street and into the driveway, and as she stopped the car, she spent a moment just staring up at the Victorian home she shared with Jan. Its beauty never ceased to amaze her, even after having lived in it for a few years, and the home brought a sense of peace each time she returned to it.

The exterior of the house was white with decorative wooden shingles. It boasted several gables, brackets under the porch roof eaves, and even a tower. There were terra cotta tiles covering the visible portion of the foundation—a few of them pictorial, with a lion's head, flowers, and an owl. There was a niche in the second-story upstairs front room below the tower—a room that Jan and Elaine shared as a living space—that made a large bay window area that presented as the base of a tower outside, with a conical peaked roof above. The front yard was full of large maple trees and plenty of flower beds that the cousins took joy in nurturing in the spring. The generous front porch wrapped around from the front side of the house to the left, and had railings with turned spindles. Out back, there was a small screened-in porch opening onto a wooden stairway that went down to a deck near the water. And below the deck there was a small boat dock that summer residents used to tie up when they traveled by water to Tea for Two.

Elaine reflected on the joy she found in her work here with tea—far greater than she'd ever expected when they'd started the business. She, Jan, and Rose, one of their employees, had a lot of fun ordering new teas and creating their own blends. For the month of August the tearoom was featuring a special blend Elaine had created herself of chamomile, orange peel, and dried raspberries, along with green tea and hibiscus flowers, which reminded her of Hawaii. The custom brew was light and delicious, for those wanting a pick-me-up a little less intense than coffee or black tea.

Shaking herself out of her reverie, Elaine got out of her Malibu and went around the outside of the house into the kitchen, pausing along the way to pat Earl Grey—the large gray cat who'd made himself comfortable on their porch but didn't quite live there, exactly. She found Jan pulling a tray of her mini maple croissants out of the oven.

"I never get tired of that smell," Elaine said, happily breathing in the rich aroma.

Jan placed the tray on the counter and smiled, pulling off her oven mitts. "I'm sticking with the tried and true this morning," she said. "We've got a discerning crowd."

Elaine laughed, knowing that Jan referred to Macy Atherton, a woman in her early fifties who owned and operated Green Glade Cottages, assisted by her son and his wife. Macy could almost always find something at the tearoom to complain about. Either the tea was too cold, or a dessert was too sweet or a little chewy, but the cousins had known her long enough to realize that her sometimes curmudgeonly exterior concealed a kind, generous soul.

That morning, the tearoom was closed for an hour to host a meeting to begin preparations for the upcoming Labor Day clambake—something Elaine hoped would become a tradition. A few of the local women had started talking about it at Tea for Two about a month before, and the idea had grown and gathered mass until finally they'd all decided to officially make it happen.

But before the group arrived, Roland Nance, their electrician, was dropping by to hang the chandelier they'd recovered from the Dubois mansion, the second of a pair. They had decided to hang it in the east parlor, in addition to the one they'd hung a few months ago in the dining room, to show off the beauty of the antique piece they couldn't believe they'd found. The first one they'd rescued from a trip to the Dumpster at the Department of Public Works, and the second had been given to them by the owner of the mansion both had originally hung in. The history of the chandeliers, and their journey from a gilded mansion to the lowly public works building, was another mystery Jan and Elaine had solved, and it was nice to have such a gorgeous physical memento of their shared interest in amateur sleuthing.

"Anything I can help you with?" Elaine asked, hanging her purse on one of the chairs at the little chestnut kitchen table they shared for eating.

Jan shook her head and folded her arms across her chest, glancing at the clock. "Not a thing. Roland will be here soon, followed by the ladies, and everything's ready." She studied Elaine, who pulled out the chair and sat down. "How are the Leons doing?"

Elaine sighed. "They seem a little better. Still gun-shy—no pun intended, believe me—about living above the gallery after what happened on Sunday, but I think they'll be okay. They're strong."

"I've been racking my brain this morning, and I still have no theories about what might have happened," Jan said.

"Me neither," Elaine said. "But I'm going to a photo store in Waterville later on to get those photos developed, and I'm hoping that will give us a lead to start with while Dan works on interviewing people about the SUV. Rachel and Elsa gave him the visitor sign-in book from Saturday, but it stands to reason that people operating outside of the law wouldn't have signed in even if they had been at the opening day exhibit."

"True," Jan agreed, coming over to the table to sit across from Elaine. "I still think it's possible that Hattie may have misplaced her bear, so the money part is the weirdest thing, in my opinion."

"You don't think she's telling the truth?" Elaine asked.

"It's not that," Jan said. "It's just that she's so young—probably only six or so—and you know as well as I do how small children are. Maybe she did pick it up on their way out of the exhibit, and just dropped it in the excitement. Or maybe she took it into the restroom and accidentally left it there."

Elaine pondered her cousin's ideas, but for some reason, she just couldn't get on the same page. "In most cases, I would say you're absolutely right," she said. "But Hattie seems...I don't know...wise for her age. An old soul, somehow. You saw how she handled the news that her bear had gone missing. Many little ones would throw a tantrum at the news that they'd lost their most beloved possession, but she was so contained. I think I believe her."

Jan nodded, seeming to understand Elaine's rationale. "Still, if that's the case, why would anyone else want a worn-out old bear?"

"That's the question of the day, isn't it?" Elaine asked, smiling. "Maybe it's an antique or something, and Jessica just isn't aware."

"You could ask Nathan about it," Jan suggested, "if Dan will give you a copy of the bear's photo." Nathan Culver, Elaine's beau, was also an auctioneer with significant expertise in antiques.

"Good idea," Elaine said. "In the meantime, do you want to go to the photo shop with me this afternoon?"

"Sure," she said. "I've been in the kitchen all morning, and it's going to be a busy day in the tearoom. I'll probably need a break by then."

"Especially after a meeting with Macy," Elaine said. She and Jan giggled with good humor. "I wonder what crazy ideas the girls will be able to get by her."

They were interrupted by the doorbell ringing and Jan got up to answer. It was Roland, and he made quick work of hanging the chandelier in the east parlor. After he'd left, Elaine and Jan stared at the beautiful fixture for a moment. It shimmered in the sunlight, and Elaine and Jan exchanged satisfied smiles.

An hour and a half later, the clambake meeting was drawing to a close in the west parlor of Tea for Two, and Jan was pleased to see that so far, it had gone off without a hitch. Kate

Pierce, the owner of Kate's Diner, had come and offered to do most of the catering, along with Bianca Stadler from the Pine Tree Grill. Kimi from the Odyssey restaurant offered to provide the beverages and knew the name of a successful local-run clam digging company. And, of course, Macy was there— mostly out of curiosity, Jan suspected, but she knew their persnickety patron and friend would help out.

"I move to adjourn this meeting," Macy pronounced, standing up from her chair.

Macy wore navy-blue slacks and a nice blouse, and Jan could tell she'd taken care dressing for the event. As challenging as her personality could be sometimes, Macy was a fixture in their town, and Jan couldn't imagine it without her. She had to agree with Macy's suggestion to wrap up the meeting. Through the large window behind the owner of Green Glade, looking out onto the front porch, Jan could see a blue sky and a glorious swath of sunshine. She'd never say so, but she couldn't wait to get out of the tearoom and into the beautiful day. She was glad she'd agreed to go to Waterville with Elaine.

"Macy, hon'," Bianca said from the chair next to Macy's, "I don't think this meeting is all that formal."

Bianca was smiling sweetly, her long brown hair and makeup done up, and her arms full of jangly gold bracelets. Jan didn't have to glance under the table to know that Bianca's feet would be clad in cowboy boots. If she didn't know better, Jan might have guessed that Bianca and her brother, Mel, who co-owned the Pine Tree Grill with her, had been born wearing boots.

"That's okay," Elaine said, standing too. "Macy's right. I think we're done for today."

The meeting had gone well, and everyone had clear tasks to work on for the next one. It would be a feat to get all the details of the clambake together in time for Labor Day, but if anyone could do it, it was the women around that table.

"Does anyone have any questions for next time?" Elaine asked.

"I do," Macy said. "What's all this about a break-in at the Heroes of Foreign Wars exhibit?"

"I meant to ask about that as well," Kate chimed in, her dark eyes curious.

"I heard that a gun went off," Kimi added.

Jan eyed Elaine across the table. News traveled fast in a small town.

Jan cleared her throat. "We don't know much," she said, glancing around the table, "but the police are working hard to find the people who broke in."

Elaine nodded. They both knew it was best to keep the details to themselves for now.

"Of course you two were there," Macy said. "You should just go on ahead and join law enforcement—you've solved more cases than they have, after all."

Good-natured laughter rumbled around the table.

"So, there was more than one bad guy?" Bianca asked, putting a hand over her heart.

"Trooper Benson thinks there may have been," Elaine answered. "But we don't know much more than that at this point. Just that Rachel and Elsa are okay, and there's an officer assigned to the gallery day and night until whoever broke in is caught."

"If you two are involved, it won't be long," Kate said, winking at Jan.

"That's the plan," Elaine said.

"Speaking of," Jan said. "Does anybody know anyone who drives a dark SUV?"

"Why?" Macy asked, her features betraying her curiosity. "Is that what the perpetrator was driving?"

Jan looked up to see Elaine rubbing her forehead in exasperation. Sometimes getting information came at a cost. She would just have to encourage the group not to get too excited.

"Not necessarily," she and Elaine said at the same time. They grinned at each other. "It's just a possibility."

"Those big ol' vehicles are a dime a dozen these days," Bianca chimed in. "Would be pretty hard to narrow it down, even in a town our size."

"You're absolutely right," Jan said, "but I figured I'd ask anyway."

"You know," Kate said, "I think the last person I saw driving one of those was Zale Atherton."

"It's true," Macy said. "She got a used one recently after her old car died. But there's no way Zale broke into the art gallery, and she sure didn't shoot the place up." Macy waved a dismissive hand.

Jan nodded, trying to ignore the *shoot the place up* comment, when there had been only one bullet hole. Sometimes small-town news was like the telephone game—it grew as it got passed along. At any rate, Macy was almost certainly correct, but if there was one thing Jan had learned after working with Elaine and Dan on several local crimes, it was not to underestimate anybody. If a person had a strong enough motive, many unexpected things were possible. She filed the information away in her mind.

The meeting wrapped up and the cousins cleared the parlor for the soon-to-arrive breakfast crowd. It would be a challenge to keep rumors surrounding the break-in from starting, but thankfully the tearoom was a hub of local talk, so maybe she and Elaine could rein it in, or at least prevent anything ridiculously untrue from spreading.

More importantly, though, they needed to catch a lead. As much as she'd like to forget it, there was a gun-wielding intruder on the loose—one who wasn't afraid to discharge his or her weapon.

Jan just prayed that person wasn't also a killer.

CHAPTER FOUR

So, if I know you, and I think I do," Elaine said, grinning at Jan in the passenger seat as she drove along the highway to Waterville after work, "you're wondering if Zale is capable of breaking into the art gallery, taking a teddy bear, and shooting a hole in the wall."

Jan tilted her head. "You know as well as I do that just about anything's possible, but to answer your question, no, I do not think that's what happened."

Elaine glanced over at her cousin as they neared town and drove past the docks. There was something odd in Jan's voice. "You don't sound entirely convinced."

"It's not that," Jan said. "I just really hope she had nothing to do with the break-in. Macy would never let us live it down if we had to investigate her daughter-in-law."

"You've got a point there," Elaine agreed. "But I really doubt we'll have to. Lots of people drive SUVs."

"Maybe it's only stuck in my craw because it's the only thing we've got so far that we're actually able to look into."

"Except the photos, of course," Elaine said hopefully.

"If there even are any real photos on that camera," Jan said. "Could be just a couple of blurry blobs."

"Could be," Elaine said. "But if blurry blobs are all we've got to go on, we'll just have to start there."

Jan giggled.

"I think the photo shop is just up here," Elaine said, peering out the window as the GPS told her to turn right.

Downtown Waterville was charming, with cute little boutiques offering clothing, furniture, jewelry, locally made products, toys, and books, and an array of dining options from southern Creole and Mexican cuisine to pub fare and fresh seafood. Elaine and Nathan sometimes liked to grab lunch there, especially at this time of year when the weather was nice and they could sit outdoors.

Today, though, she and Jan had a task to complete, and she said a silent prayer that their trip to the photo shop would be productive and would lead to a clue of some sort.

"Here we are," Elaine said, pulling into a parking space along a main downtown street. She and Jan got out of the car and walked into a building with Old-Fashioned Drugstore painted on a little hanging sign out front, underneath a red-and-white striped awning. The building itself was brick and had two narrow windows on the top floor like eyes. When she opened the door and stood aside to let Jan in, a bell chimed invitingly.

"Afternoon, ladies," came a cheerful voice from the counter near the door.

Elaine turned to see a man about her and Jan's age with salt-and-pepper hair and twinkling gray eyes.

"Can I help you with something?" he asked. His name tag indicated he was the manager.

"We're looking for the photo shop," Jan said, offering a smile in greeting.

"Ah," the manager answered. "Just head straight toward the back and Jessica will help you out." He smiled back at the cousins, obviously eager to help.

"Thanks so much," Elaine said. "You have a lovely shop here."

The manager beamed and nodded as they continued deeper into the store. It held the same items as any modern pharmacy, but was decorated with old-fashioned apothecary items on the walls, and a large curio cabinet near a middle aisle held several antique tonics and ointments, as well as bars of soap and pretty cold cream jars made of sea glass.

When they got to the photo department, Elaine pushed the little bell on the counter.

"Those always bother me," she said to Jan, who stood nearby, checking out a display of film. "They sound so demanding."

"They don't bug me," came a woman's voice. "If we didn't have one, I'd lose customers since I spend so much time in the back."

"Jessica!" Elaine greeted. "I had no idea we'd find you here."

Jessica Lachlan smiled at them both as Jan turned from the film shelf.

"Well, hello there!" Jan said cheerfully. "The manager did say Jessica. We just didn't know it would be this one."

Elaine and Jessica grinned.

"What can I help you with?" Hattie's mother asked, placing her hands on the counter.

"Actually," Elaine began, "I've got a camera here with a couple of pictures on it—literally two—but it's a bit on the older side. I read online that your shop is wonderful at handling film, and this could be too important to take to just any drugstore."

"Well, I'm intrigued," Jessica said.

Elaine noticed that Jessica's hair was pulled back into a neat chignon at the base of her neck today, rather than the ponytail she'd worn at the exhibit, and her lovely brown eyes had just a hint of purple underneath them. She must not have been sleeping well, Elaine thought sadly, remembering Pastor Mike's comment that Jessica worked long hours to cover the rent on the small house she shared with Hattie. Elaine couldn't help but wonder why the little girl's father didn't appear to be helping out.

"It's a funny coincidence to meet you here," Jan said, "because these photos—if they're anything usable—could help us find out what happened at the gallery."

Jessica's eyes widened and she tucked her hands into the pockets of the lavender cardigan she wore over a white shirt with jeans. "I still can't believe such a thing happened in Lancaster. I haven't lived there for very long, but it seems like such a safe place. The idea of a guy running around with a gun and bad intentions doesn't sit well with me. I read about it in the paper this morning and it seems like they don't have much to go on."

"Not yet, anyway," Elaine soothed. "I can't blame you for being nervous. Especially when you've got a little one to think of. But I can assure you the police will do everything they can to catch whoever broke in, and we'll help too."

Jessica smiled and her eyes brightened a little. "I've heard about your sleuthing skills," she said, "and I'm glad to have you on the case."

"We want to help find Hattie's bear as much as we want to find out who broke in," Jan added.

Jessica smiled. "She's been so torn up about that bear, but the article said a gunshot had gone off in the gallery, so catching the shooter is much more important."

"Well," Elaine said, "hopefully we can get to the bottom of both."

"Let's take a look at that camera," Jessica said, reaching out an open hand.

Elaine passed Ben's camera over the counter, pointing to the little ticker that showed two photographs had been taken.

Jessica frowned. "Only two, just like you mentioned."

"Yes," Elaine answered. "But these seem to have been taken—possibly accidentally, though I can't yet know for sure—on the night of the break-in."

"Oh," Jessica said, understanding. "I see. So they might have something in them that the police could use?"

"Yes," Elaine said. "That's what we're hoping anyway."

Jessica met Elaine's eyes. "Unfortunately, in that case, I have some bad news. You see, this film is aged and, while it's not too old for me to develop here in the store, I'm concerned that it wouldn't have the very best chance of coming out as clearly as possible."

Elaine's expression must have shown her confusion.

"We take every precaution to develop film to the highest quality here, but we don't have the equipment a developer will need for a job this important. It's a little complicated to explain but, basically, there are a lot of things that can go wrong in the development process, and with these being possibly very significant photos, I just don't want to take that risk," Jessica explained. "There are several factors that determine whether or not an old roll of film will turn out well, and it can't be assumed that just because the film is only a few decades old that the photos will come out clear."

"Do you know anyone who would have that kind of equipment?" Jan asked.

"Yes, and he's wonderful," Jessica said, reaching behind the counter for a piece of notepaper and a pen. She scrawled down a name, phone number, and website before handing the sheet over to Elaine. "Just give Howard a call and I know he'll be able to help you. He works out of his home here in Waterville, and he's been at it for a very long time. He's the best specialist I know of, and he's very kind and easy to work with. I'm so sorry I'm not able to help you more, but this film deserves caution." Jessica handed the camera back to Elaine.

"That's perfectly all right," Elaine reassured her. "You've been very helpful anyway. I wouldn't have known where else to start."

Jessica smiled softly and Elaine turned to leave, Jan beside her, before she thought of something and stopped.

"I don't want to bother you, but would it be okay if I dropped by sometime just to say hello? I'd love to bring Hattie some of our cookies," Elaine asked.

"That sounds nice," Jessica said warmly. "I'm in the pink house on Maple Street. Come any time. Hattie and I would love to have you."

It was a sweet welcome, Elaine thought, especially since she got the sense that Jessica was very busy and her time with her daughter, precious.

"Wonderful," Elaine said out loud, silenty giving a prayer of thanks. If God would use her to make this young mother a little less lonesome in her new town, Elaine would do so with joy. Everyone needed a community, she thought, recalling from her extensive travels with Ben's military career exactly how it felt to be the new person in a strange place.

In the meantime, she would help by going to see Howard, and figuring out what happened in that gallery.

CHAPTER FIVE

Elaine woke early the next morning and made herself a cup of English Breakfast in the kitchen. She added a little milk and sugar before carrying it upstairs to the sitting room. She went back to her bedroom and grabbed her laptop, then brought it in as well, making herself comfortable on the window seat.

The sun had not yet begun to rise and the room was a little cool, so she pulled her robe around her. After some quiet time and prayer, Elaine opened her laptop to search for the photo specialist.

"Howard Plushnik," she read aloud from the piece of notepaper Jessica had given her the day before. She typed in his website address and was greeted with a nice-looking but simple home page, with an easy-to-navigate layout. The bio said Mr. Plushnik had been a freelance photojournalist before retiring, and a quick glance at the magazines he'd worked for was impressive. He must have been very successful. Reading along, Elaine discovered he'd left behind the crazy schedule and frequent travel to start his own business, learning everything he could about developing old and odd film. Clicking around, she browsed through an extremely thorough frequently asked questions page, and then landed on the reviews he'd posted. After reading just a few, Elaine decided she didn't need any more convincing—Howard looked like just the man for the job. She wrote down his home address, which also served as his business, as Jessica had mentioned, before clicking away and opening her e-mail.

She brushed past some junk mail before her eyes landed on something from her daughter Sasha. Elaine took a sip of her tea, closing her eyes at the delicious warmth, wanting to savor the beverage before savoring the e-mail. She had two grown children: Jared, her eldest, was in his early thirties and lived in Ohio with his wife, Corinne, and their young kids, Lucy and Micah. Sasha, who was in her late twenties, had previously lived in Colorado and worked as a fitness trainer at a gym in a ski resort, but, joy of joys, had recently decided to live closer to her mother and boyfriend, Brody, and was now renting an apartment in Lancaster.

After clicking on the e-mail, Elaine read a few lines. Sasha wanted to spend some time with her mother and Nathan, and bring Brody along. Perhaps they could all go out to dinner together somewhere, including Jan and her boyfriend, Bob Claybrook. It would be so much fun; she could spend some time later that day looking for a good place to eat that they would all enjoy. Perhaps she'd speak with her cousin and they could invite Jan's kids along too. Brian had a birthday coming up if memory served, and she would love to hear how Amy's pregnancy was going and ask after Tara's growing jewelry business.

The e-mail was perfectly cheerful, but something about the way Sasha was emphasizing being together and enjoying things struck Elaine as odd, as if Sasha's words were a little forced. Could she be missing her friends in Colorado already? Surely not. She'd been thrilled to be able to move here near her mom and Brody. No, she was imagining things, Elaine decided. No need to borrow trouble.

When she'd responded to Sasha's e-mail with a promise to call as soon as she could so the two of them could make plans, Elaine closed her laptop lid and grabbed the computer and her mug before heading to her bedroom to get ready for the day.

A little while later, she bounded down the stairs and found Jan sitting at the kitchen table, eating toast. "That looks good," she said, eyeing Jan's breakfast.

"The bread and jam are still out—butter's in the fridge," Jan said. "And good morning, by the way," she said, winking.

"Good morning to you too," Elaine responded with a wry smile. "Sorry! I was distracted. I got an e-mail from Sasha and she wants us to go to dinner with her and Brody this week-end—Nathan and Bob too. We haven't made any plans yet, so I was thinking we could see if Tara and Jack, Amy and Van, and Brian and Paula might want to join in."

"That sounds great! I can put the word out and see what they think. And it's wonderful to see Sasha in love," Jan commented.

"Yes, it is," Elaine agreed, pulling out two slices of bread to pop into the toaster. "It will be even more wonderful for her when Brody proposes."

"You think it might happen soon?" Jan asked.

Elaine leaned against the counter. "I do, yeah," she said. "They get along great and I think they'll make a good pair."

"Makes sense," Jan said before taking a sip of her morning tea.

Elaine's toast popped up with a loud sound and she pulled out the two slices of bread and dropped them onto a plate, which she set on the place mat across from Jan. Then she went to grab the butter, jam, and a knife.

The kitchen at Tea for Two was large and well-stocked. It had a sizeable island with cupboards underneath, granite countertops, and a baking station for Jan, to make it easier for her to get to the ingredients she used frequently. The stainless steel refrigerator was extra large and boasted french doors, and the cabinets were made of rich walnut. The little window over the sink boasted pretty lace curtains, and there was a bright-blue bowl near the coffeemaker that they kept full of lemons to add a splash of color. The room was warm, functional, and cozy, and Jan spent most of her time there while Elaine had a small office just off it for managing the books and other business.

"Did you find out anything more about Howard, the guy who develops old film?" Jan asked before taking another sip of her tea.

Elaine nodded, her mouth full of toast.

"Mind if I come along today?" Jan asked. "I'm curious to meet him, and Archie and Rose will both be here this morning." Archie Bentham was their other employee. He and Rose were as close to Jan and Elaine as family and just as reliable.

"Sure. He seems like a really interesting guy—I checked out his website this morning and it seems like he really knows his stuff."

"Good," Jan said. "I can't wait to find out what's in those photos."

They finished the rest of their breakfast, sharing ideas about where they might want to take Sasha and Brody and the others.

"Ask Bob if he'd like to come along," Elaine urged. "I'm sure Nathan would be glad for his company too."

Bob was an attorney who had recently moved back to Lancaster after working in Baltimore for a spell. Jan had been through a hard time when he'd left to pursue a dream job, and the long-distance relationship had been a challenge, but she was happy as a clam to have him back.

Nathan Culver owned an auction house in Waterville and specialized in antiques. Not only was he handsome—lean with light brown, gray-sprinkled hair and blue eyes—but his talent and experience had also come in handy on several occasions when Elaine and Jan needed help solving a case involving old objects. Elaine and Nathan had been childhood friends and rekindled their relationship when Elaine moved back to Lancaster to start the tearoom with Jan.

"I'll ask him," Jan said. "Sounds like fun."

The cousins finished eating and cleared their plates before putting them in the dishwasher to run later. While Jan wrote down for Rose and Archie what baked goods she wanted them to serve that day, and what tea blends should go alongside,

Elaine called ahead to see if Howard was available to meet with them that morning.

"All set?" Jan asked when Elaine had finished her phone call.

"He said we could come by anytime, and I told him it would be about a half hour."

"We oldies are up so early," Jan said, smiling.

"It's the best time of day, if you ask me," Elaine said. "Besides, a little bird told me this is the best way to catch the worm."

Laughing at her silly joke, the two women grabbed their purses and light sweaters for the cool morning air. Elaine tucked Ben's camera into her bag and they headed outside to her car.

"COME IN, COME in," said Howard Plushnik from his front doorway after Elaine and Jan had introduced themselves. "It's so nice to meet you."

Jan and Elaine followed Mr. Plushnik, who looked to be in his midsixties, into a small, tidy sitting room. He offered them something to drink, but they declined, letting him know they'd just come from breakfast. He motioned for them to sit at a couch, then took a leather chair that faced them.

"You have a lovely home here, Mr. Plushnik," Jan complimented. The walls of the living room were, unsurprisingly, filled with photographs in all shades—black and white, sepia-toned, and color, and Elaine was certain she'd never seen so many beautiful landscapes in her life. From all over the world, they appeared to have been his favorite subject. Ben would have been unable to sit down in that room, drawn as he'd been to skilled photography.

"Oh, please call me Howard," he said, waving away the formality. He smiled at the cousins, his brown eyes intelligent and good-natured. He had mostly gray hair which stood out against his tan skin, pleasantly weathered from years and years under the sun, and wore a simple pair of tan slacks with a white button-down shirt under a soft-looking gray sweater vest.

"Howard, then," Jan corrected. "You must have gone all over the world to take all of these." She waved a hand across the room.

"Oh yes, I certainly have," he said. "And I wouldn't trade it for anything. It was a different kind of life, but it suited me well." He looked from Jan to Elaine. "You know what they say— find something you love to do and you'll never have to work a day in your life."

"It's good advice," Elaine said, smiling.

"Now, what can I help you with?" Howard folded his hands on his knees and leaned forward, eager to hear what they would say next.

Elaine pulled the camera out of her bag and handed it to Howard. She gave him a moment to study it before explaining, "It belonged to my late husband, Ben. It was one of his favorite possessions."

"A nice piece," Howard said, nodding. "Was your husband a professional?"

She shook her head. "Not by any means, but he loved taking pictures. He saved up to buy that."

"It's a good one," Howard continued. "A very decent choice."

He turned the camera over and over in his leathery hands with interest, the way an archaeologist would a fossil. Finally, his eyes landed on the film ticker and a crease formed on his brow.

"Interesting," he observed. "Only two photos taken." He looked up at Elaine, obviously hoping for an explanation.

"Yes," she said. "That's why we're here."

She swallowed, thinking over how exactly to relay how the photos had come about.

"You see, there was a break-in at our local art gallery—in Lancaster," Jan said, helping her begin.

"Ah, yes. A nice town you have," Howard said. "I'm dreadfully sorry to hear about the gallery intrusion."

"We were too," Elaine added. "And those two photos might very well have something to do with it."

Howard's eyebrows rose. "A mystery?"

"Yes," Jan said. "Something like that. We're hoping we can help the police figure out what happened. Those photos were taken the night of the crime—intentionally or by accident, we don't know."

He looked more closely at the camera. "It does look like the button could be depressed if the camera fell. Do you know anything about what happened?"

Elaine nodded. "The gallery is having a special exhibit this week, showcasing memorabilia from heroes of foreign wars, and I contributed this camera, as my husband was a lieutenant colonel active during the Gulf War."

Howard leaned in closer, his curiosity piqued.

"The camera was in the gallery overnight when someone broke in. Somehow it was dropped or was knocked to the floor, and these pictures were on it the next morning. It had zero pictures when I left it there the previous day."

"Very, very interesting," Howard said, rubbing his chin. "So you would like for me to develop them and see what kind of evidence you've got here," he observed.

"Exactly," Elaine said.

"Well, you made a good choice in coming to me. The film for this camera isn't very old, I'm guessing."

"Maybe twenty years or so," Elaine said. "Ben bought a digital model after this one, and I suspect he probably just forgot that this roll was in here."

"*Hmm,*" Howard murmured. "A lot of people think film of that age can be developed anywhere, and in some cases, they're correct. However, in your case, I think you made the right decision by coming to see me."

He gently set the camera on the walnut coffee table between them before continuing. "The quality of expired film is highly variable, and there are many factors that can affect how it turns out. Age is a big one, of course, but it's not safe to assume that newer film will turn out better than older. Temperature is also significant—was this ever kept in a hot place?" he asked.

Elaine shook her head. "No. I've always been careful to keep it in a cool area, as was Ben."

"Excellent," Howard said. "Some brands are better than others, and this is a pretty good one. Humidity can be a problem, and this is Maine, so we're no stranger to that," he said, grinning. "And I could go on and on about format, processing method, light versus dark storage, et cetera—and I tend to do so sometimes, which probably would not help you ladies very much."

Elaine smiled, grateful that Jessica had referred her to someone who obviously knew an extensive amount about photography.

"You came here for my help, and I will do the very best I can. I'm assuming whoever sent you to me did so because of the high importance these pictures might have."

"Jessica Lachlan," Elaine said. "And you're absolutely right."

Howard nodded. "Jessica is great. I'll remember to thank her for passing along my name once again. Now, if the film was new and we knew every step of its history, I would say go anywhere and you'd be fine. But I can understand why you chose to work with a specialist considering the story behind these photos."

Elaine and Jan looked at each other, hopeful they would soon receive a clue that would allow them to move forward with the case.

"I do have to warn you, though I'm sure you know this already—there may very well be nothing here," he said.

"We're prepared for that," Elaine said, "but obviously we're hoping otherwise."

"I like your positivity," Howard said, smiling. "I don't have too many orders going right now, so if you can give me, say, a couple of days, I can probably have these done for you by Thursday."

"Oh, that sounds great," Elaine said, sending up a silent thank-you that it wouldn't take too long.

She hadn't known exactly what to expect, but some of the places online said two or more weeks to develop older types of film, and they just couldn't afford to wait that length of time. The exhibit might already suffer a thinner crowd because of what had happened, and on top of that Elaine didn't like the thought of Rachel and Elsa being afraid in their own home, wondering what might happen if the gunman returned.

"I'm glad," Howard responded. "Do you have any other questions before I get to work on this?" he asked.

"What do I owe you?" Elaine asked.

"Oh, nothing right now, of course," Howard said. "You only pay me if the photographs turn out to be usable."

Elaine's mouth nearly opened in surprise. "How kind of you," she said.

"No, no," Howard responded. "That's just how I work. This is not my job—it's a passion. I do it to help people who come in having found old film from loved ones and photographs that have been ruined over the years that need restoration, yes. But mostly, I do it because I love it."

"Well, thank you, Howard," Elaine said, shortly echoed by Jan.

"Thank me when you have these photos," he corrected, holding up the camera. "I'll keep my fingers crossed, but not while I'm working," he joked, causing the cousins to laugh.

"We'll look forward to seeing them," Jan said.

Howard showed them out and Jan and Elaine got back into the Malibu.

"I could use some lunch," Elaine said. "Are you up for it?"

"Definitely," Jan answered. "I think the anticipation of finding out what's on that film is making me hungry."

Elaine nodded. She couldn't agree more.

TEA FOR TWO was bustling with an afternoon crowd when Jan and Elaine returned from their visit and lunch. The cousins hadn't had much time to talk about what they knew so far, and Jan was eager for a chance to do so. Hopefully, she thought as she jumped right in to help Archie and Rose, they would have the opportunity tomorrow.

For the moment though, things were pleasantly busy. Jan had time to stop and chat with one of the Burgess teenagers. The Burgesses were a summer family from Des Moines, Iowa, and had four children. It was no wonder the young girl sitting at a corner table wanted to catch a break from all those siblings.

"Hi there," Jan said, coming up to the table. "Can I get you a refill on your iced tea?" she asked.

The girl looked up and smiled, her green eyes friendly. She had long, wavy auburn hair, pulled up into a messy bun on top of her head.

"Oh no, thank you," she answered politely. "I'm almost finished up here."

She had a notebook open in front of her, and pens of several different colors scattered all over. She'd been biting her lip as she worked, an unconscious gesture that made Jan grin.

"Are you working on something special?" Jan asked, getting the sense that the girl was social and wouldn't mind chatting for a bit.

"Yes," she said. "I'm taking an SAT course online before my junior year starts." She rolled her eyes in emphasis. "Not exactly a fun way to spend the summer, but I'm sure I'll be glad I took the course when it comes time for the test in the fall. I'm Amber, by the way."

Amber extended a hand, which Jan accepted with a smile, pleased to meet a young person with good manners.

"I'm Jan Blake," she said. "My cousin and I own this tearoom, and I hope you're enjoying your order." Jan eyed the mostly eaten slice of blueberry pie, made with fresh berries, of course, next to Amber's iced tea.

"I definitely am," Amber said. "You make the best blueberry pie I've ever had."

Jan beamed. Compliments from adults were always nice, but they carried something extra special when they came from children, who often didn't feel as much social pressure to be generous with praise.

"I'm so glad," Jan said. "Next time you come in, we'll give you a slice on the house."

"Awesome!" Amber exclaimed. "A yummy treat definitely makes the studying go better—this stuff is hard!"

"I can imagine," Jan said. "I'll leave you to it. I'm happy you stopped by. Tell your family that Mrs. Cook and I said hello, and you're all very welcome here any time."

"Will do," Amber agreed cheerfully, and Jan walked back to the kitchen with a light heart and a pep in her step to tell Rose that their pie had passed the kid test.

"I see you've made a new friend!" Archie called out as he brushed through the swinging kitchen doors carrying a tray full of empty dishes.

His thick white hair was neatly combed and his hazel eyes shone with intelligence and keen observation. Archie had been retired, but his love of tea had led him to seek employment at Tea for Two, despite being vastly overqualified. He had a wealth of knowledge about tea and serving etiquette, and charmed customers with his posh, professor-like British accent.

Jan smiled. "I enjoy all of our customers, but it is nice to have a younger person pop in, especially one so enthusiastic about our pastries." She winked at Rose.

Rose beamed. "I served Amber the other day. She's a sweetheart."

"Speaking of serving," Jan said, "would you two mind teaming up to help that group of out-of-towners who just walked in? There are at least eight and I've got to go back and top off a few teacups."

"Absolutely," Rose said, putting down the washcloth she'd been using to wipe down the countertop.

Archie finished loading his tray full of used tea service into the dishwasher, washed his hands, and hurried to join Rose.

Jan refilled her teapot and headed back out to the parlor to make a round. Out of the corner of her eye she saw Rose smiling at an elderly couple in the group as she told them about the "special-teas" of the day. Meanwhile, as Jan poured refills, she overheard Archie tell someone who'd asked about his accent, "You can take a man out of England, but you can't take the England out of the man," which caused an eruption of laughter. Her heart warmed as she thought of how dear the two employees had come to be to her and Elaine, and how thankful she was to live in such a warm, safe community.

Well, at least it would be again soon.

CHAPTER SIX

The next day was a typical summer Wednesday, busy with a steady flow of tourists eager to soak up the last month of summer before fall unofficially arrived. As the morning rush at Tea for Two began, Jan gathered the orange zest scones she'd baked earlier and placed them in a basket along with a bag of loose cranberry zinger tea, plus supplies, before loading everything into her car.

"I won't be too long," she told Elaine, who was bringing an order to an elderly member of the breakfast crowd. "I should be back before lunch."

Elaine smiled and waved her off. "Take your time," she said. "Rose, Archie, and I are all set here. Rachel and Elsa will be glad to see you."

Jan started up her car and pulled out of the drive, humming along with the music on a local classics station as she headed in the direction of the art gallery. As much as she enjoyed the warmer summer months, she was looking forward to the arrival of the fall season and all its trimmings—watching the leaves transform from green to more shades of red and gold than a painter could capture, pumpkin patches full of little children seeking out the perfect orange globe, pulling cozy sweaters out of the depths of her closet—followed, of course, by her favorite time of year: Christmas. It was always hard to say goodbye to long days full of sunshine, but celebrating the birth of Christ and spending time with family made the short, frigid days well worth it.

Jan breathed a sigh of longing for the holiday season, but then reminded herself what a gift it was to be in the moment, enjoying the bright blue sky and the feel of sunny rays on her arms.

As she drove into the art gallery parking lot, Jan gave a small wave to the officer on duty, who held up his to-go coffee cup by way of returning her greeting. She wanted to offer him a scone and a word of encouragement, but she talked herself out of it. It would only distract him. Instead, she prayed that he and the other officers who took turns guarding the gallery since the break-in would stay out of harm's way and keep the Leon sisters safe.

Jan grabbed the refreshments basket out of her car and approached the front door of the gallery, which Rachel opened for her.

"Good morning," Rachel said, her voice giving away a hint of weariness.

Jan's heart went out to her as she set the basket down on the table they'd been using for the treats. She was a little surprised, but touched, when the younger woman reached out for a brief hug.

"How are you two holding up?" Jan asked.

Rachel offered a wan smile that was kind but didn't quite reach her eyes. There were still dark smudges beneath them, and it was clear she still wasn't sleeping much. Who could blame her after what happened?

"We're doing a little bit better," Rachel answered, "but it would be dishonest if I said it was easy, or that I'm not still afraid."

"This wouldn't be easy for anyone," Jan said, her tone soothing. "But the fact that you and your sister are keeping the gallery open for the exhibit says a lot about the kind of strength you must have, and I know a lot of people are thankful." Jan looked around the gallery. "These displays mean so much to so many folks."

Rachel nodded and her features showed a little less tension. "Thank you," she said. "I appreciate your support. We wouldn't dream of closing during such an important event."

The two women worked in companionable silence for a few moments as Jan set up the large electric kettle and Rachel helped arrange the scones on a platter at the refreshments table.

"Have you heard any new information from Dan about your case?" Jan asked as they finished up and stood back to survey their work.

Rachel nodded. "Yes, a little, but it hasn't led to anything further."

Jan turned and studied the young woman, noticing the strange expression on Rachel's face—almost a half grin of amusement. "What's funny?" she couldn't help asking.

Rachel shook her head. "Oh, it's nothing. Just that, well, Dan went on for a while about the science they have now to identify bullets. I think I may have even zoned out a little and I felt bad because I know he was trying to help make me feel better about their chances of finding the gun, but I've got to tell you—a lot of it just went over my head."

Jan smiled back. "I completely understand where you're coming from. A lecture on forensic science isn't for everyone. But I'm curious anyway. Do you remember anything specific he said?" She was quite interested—she wanted to know every detail—but she didn't want to overwhelm the clearly sleep-deprived gallery owner.

Rachel bit her bottom lip in thought. "He said that gun barrels are filed when they are made."

"You mean rifled?" Jan asked.

Rachel nodded. "Yes, rifled. When they're being manufactured, the insides of the barrels are finished with rotating grooves so that bullets will spin after a shot. Apparently it makes the flight more accurate somehow, though I can't recall how. The grooves and the flat areas between them leave corresponding markings on any bullets that are shot from that particular gun, so if you fire another bullet from that same gun, the grooves of both bullets can be matched side by side, with magnification."

"Wow," Jan responded. "I had no idea. Sort of like fingerprints."

"Right," Rachel said. "Exactly. And there's more."

Jan raised her eyebrows, intrigued.

"So, even without having the exact weapon in evidence, the lab tech can use the striations to identify the type and model of a gun so that the police can have an idea of what to search for."

"I see," Jan said. "Dan mentioned that he thought the gun was some type of Glock—a fairly common handgun, but I guess that would give them a way to be certain what to look for."

"That's what he told me as well. A Glock 43, plus some size in millimeters, though I can't remember the number exactly. So if they catch the person who shot inside our gallery, and they find the weapon in their possession and it has fingerprints and such, they'll have a good idea whether that person was the one who did it."

"Makes sense," Jan said. "But I see what you mean about it not leading anywhere yet."

Rachel sighed sadly.

"Now, don't give up hope," Jan encouraged. "Often finding the solution to a case is just a matter of adding up all these tiny little clues. This one sounds like it could help lead them to a bigger find, or at least prove guilt once they catch the person. That's something—and it's worth holding on to. There will be more, trust me."

Rachel gave Jan a lopsided grin. "I'm so thankful to have you and Elaine looking into this in addition to the police. Your mystery-solving success rate is...well...no mystery."

The two women laughed.

"And speaking of clues," Jan added, "Elaine discovered that the camera of Ben's that she put on display for the exhibit seems to have inadvertently taken two photos the night of the break-in."

"Really?" Rachel asked, her eyes wide.

"Yes," Jan answered. "And we're in the process of having them developed by a specialist, so we can find out if the camera caught anything."

"Oh my," Rachel said. "There could be anything in those photos, even a picture of the criminal or criminals who broke in here."

"I don't want to get ahead of ourselves, but that's certainly what Elaine and I are hoping to find out," Jan explained.

"Oh, that's excellent," Rachel said. "I sure hope something useful will come of those pictures. Elsa and I could really use some good news."

"I know you could," Jan said. "If there is anything at all on that film, we'll share it with Dan and his team right away and see if it leads to anything."

Just then Elsa came down the stairs and Jan and Rachel caught her up on what they'd been discussing. Jan noticed that Elsa looked a little more refreshed than her sister and seemed to be taking everything in stride. Elsa was the confident and carefree one, and Rachel was the unassuming and responsible sister. Their complementary personalities made Jan smile. The sisters needed each other, and the differences God had given them were perfectly suited for helping each other out in times like this—reminding Jan of her relationship with Elaine.

The three women chatted a little longer about the case and then the success of the exhibit. "There is a bright side to all this," Elsa assured Jan with an arch smile. "Yesterday's profits tipped the scale, and we've met the goal of the purchase price for the handicapped-accessible van—far earlier than expected! The exhibit has already been a great help to the VFW, and this has all been worth it."

"Oh, Cora and the other chapter members will be so happy!" Jan exclaimed. She joined the sisters in a mini celebration with scones and cranberry tea, and finally, glancing at her watch, announced that she needed to get back to the tearoom. As they parted ways and she got back into her car, Jan said a prayer that the sisters would support each other and that there would soon be more information on the case to follow.

Her heart thankful for the new van the local VFW chapter would soon be purchasing, Jan drove back to the tearoom to pick up Elaine before heading to Jessica's house to check on her and Hattie. On the way there, the cousins spoke briefly about what they knew so far about the case, which admittedly wasn't much. But there were still possibilities to keep their hope alive.

"We've got the pictures coming soon, so that could turn up a lead," Elaine said.

"Yep, and Dan's pretty sure he knows the type and model of the gun, but of course the team hasn't yet recovered the actual weapon used to fire the bullet they found," Jan added.

"Right, so that leaves the tire tracks and the footprints, which the police are investigating, and we still don't know anything about the bag of money or the missing teddy bear," Elaine said.

Jan turned onto Pine Ridge Road. "Do you think the crimes are separate?" she asked. "I mean, do you think the money and the bear are not related?"

"I don't know," Elaine answered. "I can't see how they would be linked in any way, but it also doesn't make sense that the money would be left behind on the same night that Hattie's toy went missing, unless she really did just lose it, and I don't think that's the case here. She seems like an honest child—not one to make up stories."

"I agree," Jan said. "It's totally weird that someone would leave behind a bag of money."

"I'm guessing it wasn't intentional," Elaine said. "Remember how the bills were spilling out of the bag?"

Jan nodded, slowing down as they entered the neighborhood where Jessica lived. The homes were small cottages, each painted a different pastel color that reminded Jan of sherbet, and the street was lined with mature trees. Many of the yards had bicycles and toys out front, and Jan saw a few children playing happily in the sunshine. "Yes," she answered, "which means the person who dropped the bag most likely did so by accident."

Elaine chuckled. "That's the only way I'd leave a bunch of money behind somewhere—I sure wouldn't do it on purpose."

"True," Jan said, with a laugh. "Me neither, but then again, we don't think like criminals."

"And thank the Lord for that," Elaine said.

"This looks like the one," Jan said, pulling into the driveway of a little pink house with white rosebushes filling a bed near the front door. The roses were pleasantly unruly and made Jan smile.

"I hope she really doesn't mind us dropping in," Elaine said. "I texted earlier to see if today would be good and Jessica said she's not scheduled to work until after lunchtime and Hattie's been attending day care in the afternoons. Still, I know it must be challenging to manage everything as a single parent."

"It would certainly take a lot of strength," Jan added.

"Maybe these muffins will brighten her morning," Elaine said, pulling a basket of Jan's blueberry-lemon baked goods from the backseat, along with a thermos of freshly brewed lemon tea. "If she's anything like me, she won't be able to bite into one without feeling her spirits lift."

"That's sweet," Jan said. "I just hope Hattie's doing okay with her bear still missing. I want to figure out what happened to the little guy and return him to her."

"Me too," Elaine agreed. "Just give it a bit more time. We'll hear about those photos soon. I've been praying that they'll give us what we need to pursue whoever broke into the gallery, and I trust we'll get an answer one way or another."

Jan nodded and grabbed the thermos from Elaine before the two made their way up the sidewalk to the butter-yellow front door. Using her free hand, Jan knocked a few times and heard little footsteps a few seconds later. The door opened slowly and the cousins looked down into Hattie's grinning face.

"Hi," said the girl as her mother came up behind her.

"Well, hello there," Jan said, matching the child's grin. It was virtually impossible not to. She was just too cute.

Then Jan greeted Jessica, who pulled the door open wider as Hattie stepped behind her legs, suddenly shy.

"Good morning to you both," Jessica said, her voice light and pleasant. "Please, come on in. Try to ignore the mess."

The cousins followed Jessica down a short, narrow hallway. Despite Jessica's warning, the house didn't strike Jan as messy.

There were some toys scattered here and there, but everything was clean and obviously cared for. The walls were painted a soft beige and were decorated mostly with family photos and a landscape print here and there. When Jessica showed Jan and Elaine to the living room, Jan noticed pretty white cotton curtains adorning three picture windows, which made the small room appear open and inviting. Everywhere, it was clear that the young mother put effort into making a comfortable home for her daughter.

Jessica motioned for the cousins to sit on the couch. "Would you like me to take those and serve them?" she asked about the muffins and tea. "They look delicious."

"Yes, that would be wonderful," Elaine said. "Would you like help?"

"Oh no, you go ahead and visit with Hattie here while I get plates and cups," Jessica answered, offering a warm smile.

Jan thought that sounded like a great idea. As Jessica turned to go, Jan turned to admire a dollhouse in a corner of the living room.

"What a marvelous dollhouse you've got there," Jan said to Hattie.

"Do you want to see who lives inside?" the little girl asked, looking between Jan and Elaine, her eyes lighting up as she forgot her earlier shyness.

"Absolutely," Elaine said, and Hattie rushed over to kneel in front of the house.

She opened the front façade and began to pull out little figures from inside, sharing all of their names and showing the cousins each of their bedrooms, then the kitchen and living room. By the time Hattie had finished with the introductions, Jan and Elaine had both joined her and been assigned dolls to play with. Jan was having a great time when Jessica returned from the kitchen holding a tray.

"Here we are," she said to Jan and Elaine. "It was so nice of you to bring these." Then to Hattie, "Sweetie, wasn't that nice of Mrs. Blake and Mrs. Cook?"

"Yes, thank you," said Hattie politely, abandoning the dolls in favor of a morning treat.

Jan and Elaine followed suit, returning the little plastic people to their home before going back to sit on the couch across from a chair Jessica chose for herself. Elaine poured the tea into Jessica's white porcelain cups while Jan put muffins on four matching plates.

"How have you girls been getting along?" Jan asked, watching as Jessica spread a little butter on Hattie's muffin and then her own.

"We've been doing okay, aside from Hattie missing her bear." Jessica glanced at her daughter.

Jan couldn't put her finger on it, but something in Jessica's expression and voice was uneasy, as though maybe she wasn't doing quite as well as she'd indicated. It hadn't been present earlier when she'd greeted them at the door; perhaps Jan's question had brought on the change. She glanced at Elaine to see if her cousin had noticed, and caught a hint of recognition in the worry lines of Elaine's forehead.

Jan was about to ask if she had heard any updates from Dan when Jessica changed the subject, asking about the tearoom.

So, there was something bothering Jessica and Jan wasn't just imagining it.

"Busy as usual," Jan replied cheerfully. "Summer is our most eventful time."

Elaine caught Jan's eye before speaking to Jessica. "Have you been back to the gallery after what happened on Saturday?"

Jessica shook her head, swallowing a bite of muffin. "Goodness, these are delicious," she said.

"Those are Jan's work," Elaine said, grinning. "She's a genius in the kitchen. I place most of the tea orders, handle the books, and keep things running."

Jan chuckled. "I'm no genius. I just like to experiment."

"Well, I'd say you're a pretty good scientist if these are what happens when you experiment," Jessica complimented her.

The three women laughed. It was easy to be around Jessica, Jan thought. She was friendly and sweet. The young woman would make friends fast if she had more of a chance to spend time with other local moms. And she didn't know if Hattie had many friends or not, but there were plenty of kids her age around town. Jan made a mental note to talk to Elaine about helping Jessica and her daughter get more connected.

Jessica cleared her throat. "Elaine, were you able to get in touch with Howard?" she asked before taking a sip of tea.

"Oh yes—in fact, Jan and I visited him yesterday. He was very friendly and said the photos would be ready soon. We thought it very generous of him not to ask for payment unless they turn out well," Elaine answered.

Jessica nodded, smiling. "He's the best I know. If he's unable to handle an important project, it's probably just not possible. I'm glad he'll be able to help you."

"We're anxious to find out what's in those snapshots," Jan added. "And we're hoping it will help us find out what happened to your bear, Hattie."

The little girl smiled. "His name is Aaron," she said proudly.

Jan glanced at Jessica and caught an unmistakable spark of sadness in her eyes.

"He's named after my father," Jessica explained. "He served during the Gulf War with my uncle, Cameron."

"I remember you saying that when we met at the gallery on Saturday," Elaine said. "You said your father sent the bear home to your mother with your uncle?"

"Yes," Jessica said, nodding. "It was a gift to my mother, who was pregnant with me at the time. I think he was holding on to it until she actually gave birth, but he never made it home."

"I'm so sorry to hear that," Jan said softly.

"Thank you," Jessica said, her eyes filled with warmth. "I never got to know my dad, but Uncle Cameron has been like a father to me since I lost my own."

"Is he the one who's here in town visiting you?" Elaine asked.

Jan recalled that Cameron hadn't been with Jessica and Hattie when they'd returned to the gallery to look for the bear, and he wasn't with them now.

"Yes," Jessica said, not explaining further, her expression returning to the same worried look Jan had noticed earlier when Elaine had first asked if she had been back to the gallery.

"Is he staying with you?" Jan asked tentatively. She didn't want to be too nosy, but at the same time she had to figure out if there was something Jessica needed help with and was maybe too worried to ask.

Jan must have landed on something significant because the color suddenly drained from the young woman's cheeks. A moment passed in which everyone was silent, even Hattie, and the whole room fell still.

"Actually," Jessica began before swallowing, "he was, until Saturday."

"Is everything okay?" Elaine asked, setting her teacup on the coffee table between the couch and chair.

Jessica's hand shook against the handle of her own cup. "No, it's not," she said, looking slightly relieved that someone had asked. "He's been...missing...since that day."

Elaine and Jan shared a worried glance.

Jessica's eyes shot to a series of three photographs on the wall before she met the cousins' eyes in turn. She pulled in a deep breath. "I'm starting to think that he's in trouble."

CHAPTER SEVEN

In trouble?" Elaine asked, moving to the edge of the couch to hear better.

Jessica nodded. "He was with us—Hattie and me—on Saturday. We all went to the Heroes of Foreign Wars exhibit together to see Hattie's bear and a few photographs and things I'd lent them that belonged to my father and uncle."

Jan and Elaine listened intently. Elaine's heart was beating faster as she realized there might be more to the missing bear than they'd first thought.

"Have you seen him at all since then?" Jan asked.

Elaine could feel that her cousin's tension matched her own. Jessica shook her head *no* and sweet Hattie, sensing her mother's worry, tucked a hand into Jessica's.

Elaine hesitated before asking, "Have you told Trooper Benson about your uncle?"

Again, Jessica shook her head, and Elaine's heart lurched. Before she had a chance to insist that it would be a good idea to file a missing persons report, Jessica continued.

"I know I need to report him not coming home, but, you see, he's got a history of wandering off for a day or two here and there. He always returns, so I assumed he would this time as well, but he hasn't come back yet."

Elaine could see the young woman's concern rising as Jessica explained.

"He has PTSD, and I haven't seen him drinking—he doesn't do it around Hattie and me—but I think he might have a tendency to self-medicate when he has a flashback."

Elaine nodded. "I understand." And she meant it.

Though Ben had never fallen prey to it, PTSD and the often-resulting alcohol abuse had certainly affected more than a few of the military families they'd known.

"Uncle Cam goes to bars sometimes, and he doesn't want me to know about it," Jessica went on. "But I've checked all the ones nearby, and nobody has seen him. I've urged him to get help, but he always promises he's okay."

Elaine wanted to ask if it was possible that Cameron may have broken into the gallery during an episode, even if he couldn't remember it, but she sensed it wasn't the time to do so. However, Jessica must have seen the question in her eyes.

"I know what you're thinking," Jessica said, staring down into what was left of her tea. "But he couldn't have been the one to break into the gallery. I know this...looks bad, but he couldn't have done something like that. Besides, he wouldn't have taken the bear because he knows how much it means to Hattie."

He might not have taken the bear, Elaine thought, but that didn't mean he hadn't been the one to fire the gun or leave the money behind. Also you never knew—people did very surprising things sometimes.

"I know it's not what you want to hear, Jessica," Jan said gently, "but you must tell Trooper Benson about this. You've got to make sure that your uncle isn't hurt somewhere."

Jessica nodded, appearing on the edge of tears. "I know," she said. "I really do."

"Would you like us to stay with you while you make the call?" Elaine asked gently.

Jessica gave Elaine a soft, sad smile. "That would be nice," she said.

Elaine gave Jan a quick nod.

"Hattie, dear—why don't you and I go play with that dollhouse of yours some more?" Jan asked, reaching out a hand to the child.

Hattie took it happily and bounced off toward her toys, tugging Jan behind.

Elaine sat with Jessica while she made the call to Dan, eagerly answering his questions about Cameron's information. At the end, Jessica promised to go by Dan's office to file an official report and to bring a recent photograph of her uncle. Elaine warmed Jessica's tea in the kitchen and brought it to her where she still sat in the living room chair, disconnecting the call.

"Do you think he'll be okay?" Jessica asked, accepting the teacup.

Elaine smiled and sat down across from her. "I believe he will," she said. "I trust that God will look out for him wherever he is and that Dan has the skills needed to find him."

Jessica gave a tight-lipped smile. "I hope you're right," she said. "This isn't the first time this has happened and I really thought he would be back by now."

Elaine patted Jessica's arm. "I understand," she said. "But it's okay to ask for help. And even when Cameron comes home and all is well, you're always, always welcome to ask Jan or me for help. We're here for you."

"Thank you," she said. "That means a lot. Everyone in town has been so nice to me and Hattie. I guess I've just been so busy with work and taking care of Hattie, I haven't had time to make friends."

Elaine smiled. "Well, you've got two already," she said.

Jessica's color had returned a little, and she sat quietly for a moment, sipping her newly warmed tea. "I just want him to come home soon," she said. "I've already lost my mom and dad. I couldn't stand to lose Uncle Cameron too."

When they got back inside the Camry and buckled up, the empty thermos and muffin container in Elaine's lap, the cousins sat quietly for several seconds before either of them could speak.

"I can't believe Jessica hadn't told the police her uncle was missing until today," Jan said. "Cameron Lachlan could be in a lot of danger and nobody has been looking for him."

"Well, she did say she'd been around to bars asking about him, but I feel the same way. I understand her thought process, especially if he's done this before and there is a pattern, but I agree that she should have reported his disappearance much sooner," Elaine said.

"Maybe Jessica thought that doing so would make it all too real. She sounds like she honestly expected her uncle to have come back to her house by now," Jan added.

"Whatever her reasons," Elaine continued, "I just hope the delay hasn't put him in harm's way."

"Do you think he might have had something to do with the break-in at the gallery?" Jan asked, putting words to Elaine's next thought.

"It's possible," Elaine answered. "But what reason would he have to break in? He's a veteran himself, so I imagine he was just at the exhibit to see the memorabilia, and maybe meet some fellow soldiers. Why would he want to break in later that night?"

"That's the big question, isn't it?" Jan mused. "I guess he could have seen something he wanted and gone back to take it?"

Elaine bit her lip. "I guess so, but I didn't see anything valuable, did you?"

Jan shook her head before turning her key in the ignition. "No, I didn't. And from what we saw at the scene of the crime, whoever was there left the most valuable thing in the room—"

"The bag full of money," Elaine said, finishing Jan's thought.

"Yep," Jan agreed. "And even if he did break in and leave the money—which I still don't understand—why would he have taken the bear?"

"Well, you saw how adamant Jessica was that he wouldn't have done such a thing, knowing how much Hattie loves her teddy," Elaine said.

"Right. And anyway, he brought it all the way back to his niece from a war zone," Jan said.

"It doesn't add up," Elaine sighed.

"That's the trouble," Jan agreed. "But we've got to figure out a way to *make* it make sense."

Elaine's phone vibrated in her purse, but by the time she dug it out, it had stopped.

"It was Howard," Elaine explained, watching the screen for a voice mail notification. As soon as it came up, she clicked to listen.

When she'd finished, she reported, "He says he tried reaching me once before but I didn't pick up." She'd turned her phone to silent while they visited with Jessica.

She pushed another button. "I also missed a call from Sasha, but she left a text. She says she has a Skype date with a friend from Colorado but she'll call back later with more details about dinner plans."

"So, what else did Howard say?" Jan asked, pulling off Main Street and into the driveway of Tea for Two.

Elaine could see by the number of cars that the tearoom was busy and Archie and Rose must have their hands full.

"He had good news," Elaine answered. "He said the photos are ready and we can pick them up as soon as we're able."

"Oh, that's great!" Jan said, stopping the car. She pulled off her seat belt as Elaine put her phone away and handed Jan her purse. "Did he say what was in the photos?"

"Sorry—no," Elaine said, shaking her head. "He just left a short message. But we'll know soon enough. We could head to Waterville after closing tomorrow. I can't wait to see what's in those pictures."

LATER THAT EVENING, Elaine settled down alone in the upstairs sitting room. Something had been bothering her that afternoon, and neither a hot bubble bath nor a steaming cup of raspberry mango tea had done anything to soothe her. Finally, as she tucked her legs under her on the sofa and spread an afghan over her lap, she realized what it was.

The message from Sasha. The "Skype date with a friend from Colorado."

Elaine frowned. It was possible that Sasha referred to a gal pal, but something about the term *date* made Elaine think otherwise. She knew her daughter, and if Sasha had meant she was chatting with a friend, she would have said just that—chatting. On the other hand, she thought things were going well with her daughter and Brody, so why on earth would Sasha be "dating" someone else, even via video conference? It just didn't add up and had gotten under her skin. Deciding to do something about it, she picked up her cell phone and dialed Sasha's number.

"Hey, Mom," came her daughter's voice over the phone.

Elaine noticed instantly that Sasha didn't sound her usual self.

"Hi, sweetie," she said tentatively. "I know it's getting late, but do you have time to come by for a little bit? Just an hour or so."

Elaine's heart beat quickly as she waited for a response. For several long seconds, her daughter was quiet on the line.

Finally Sasha spoke. "Sure, Mom," she said. "Let me just finish up a load of laundry and I'll be right over." She paused. "Is everything okay?"

"Oh yes, fine," Elaine responded, though really that's exactly what she hoped to find out. "I'd just enjoy your company."

"Okay," Sasha said. "See you soon."

Half an hour later, Elaine greeted her daughter at the front door, offered her a cup of tea, and led her upstairs to the sitting room, where they both sat down on the couch.

"Where's Jan?" Sasha asked, craning her neck to see down the hallway.

"Oh, I think she's working on the computer in her bedroom," Elaine said. "Catching up on e-mails."

Sasha smiled, her blue eyes wide in the lamplit room, and Elaine thought for the umpteenth time just how pretty her young daughter was. She had rosy cheeks from her deep love of the outdoors, and shiny hair the color of nutmeg. "It's really nice to be able to just pop over and see you live and in person these days," Sasha said with a wink.

But something wasn't right, and Elaine could feel tension as she always had been able to when anything was upsetting her girl. The mother-daughter bond was strong.

"So, what did you want to talk to me about, Mom?" Sasha asked, pulling her hair into a bunch and flipping it over her shoulder. She was trying to seem relaxed, but it wasn't too convincing.

Elaine took a deep breath, taking her time in choosing the right words. She didn't want to pry, and she didn't want to make Sasha uncomfortable, but she had to know what was going on with that "date."

"How are things with Brody?" she asked, offering an open smile. With kids, no matter how old they were, she had learned that it was always better to ask than to assume.

And there it was. Sasha's eyes went wide. She seemed to be carefully deciding what to say, but then her features softened and her shoulders slumped down.

"How did you know something wasn't right?" she asked.

Elaine reached out and squeezed her daughter's hand. "Just a mother's instinct," she said. "Do you want to talk about it?" Though she hoped the answer would be yes, she would give Sasha space if that was what she needed most.

"I guess," Sasha said, pulling in a deep breath.

Elaine patted her hand before pulling the afghan over both of them.

"One of Brody's friends found out the other day that his wife is having a baby," Sasha began, holding out a palm.

"Oh, that's wonderful!" Elaine exclaimed, clasping her hands together. "New babies are always so exciting to me."

Sasha grinned from ear to ear at her mom's statement. "I know, right?" she said. "That's how I feel too." Her face fell. "And I said as much to Brody, but then we got to talking on that subject."

"About babies?" Elaine clarified, her heart sinking at the direction she thought their conversation might be headed.

Sasha nodded. "About babies. We've been dating for a while now, obviously, but this was actually the first time the subject had popped up between us. When Brody didn't seem too excited for his friend, I got the feeling there was more to it, so I asked him how many kids he wanted."

Sasha looked down at her lap and began anxiously rolling a piece of the afghan fringe between her thumb and forefinger.

"And what was his answer?" Elaine couldn't help but ask, though she could sense it wouldn't be a good one.

Her daughter looked up and Elaine noticed moisture in her eyes.

"He said he wasn't sure he wanted any at all," Sasha said.

"Oh, honey."

"I know. I guess I never expected that from him. He's such a good guy—loving and kind and generous—that I never even considered he might feel that way," Sasha said. "I don't want to pressure him to change his mind, but at the same time, I can't stay involved with someone who has such different ideas about the future."

Elaine nodded and was quiet for several moments, thinking, even as her heart ached for her daughter—a girl who had wanted a child since she'd been one herself.

"I know you're upset and you might need time to think about this...development, but you said that Brody told you he wasn't sure he wanted children—not that he *definitely* doesn't, isn't that right?" Elaine asked.

Sasha nodded slowly. "I didn't talk to him much more about it after he said that. I was too upset and I just needed to go off on my own and have some time to figure out how to respond."

Elaine nodded sympathetically. "That's perfectly reasonable," she said. "But when you've had time, and you're ready, don't you think you two should talk more about it? It sounds like he needs a chance to explain further."

"Well, before I went home that day, he did say that he doesn't know if he would be a good father or not," Sasha explained, her voice cracking slightly.

"Maybe he just needs a chance to talk it out with you," Elaine said gently. "As you know, his mother and father didn't have the greatest relationship when Brody was growing up."

Sasha looked up, her eyes narrowed in concentration. "That's true," she said. "I was so sad when I heard him say he wasn't sure he wanted a family that I didn't stop to think about what his was like." She let go of the afghan fringe.

"I remember when you and Jan and I first met Brody's mom, she mentioned that Brody's father wasn't always honest, and that eventually they'd parted ways because of that dishonesty."

"She called him 'unreliable,' if I remember correctly." Sasha nodded. "Yeah. Brody doesn't talk about it much, but I know from what he has mentioned that his parents fought a lot and things between them were pretty uncomfortable at times. And I got the impression that his dad didn't always treat his mom very well."

"I'm sorry to hear that," Elaine said softly. "That can really affect the way a child views parenting."

"I know, Mom," Sasha said. "I hadn't thought of it that way, but if most of what he saw growing up was fighting and arguing, he might not think it seems like much fun to raise a child in such an environment."

"That's very possible," Elaine agreed. "We can't make assumptions about how he feels, and of course you will have to talk to him, but it could be that he thinks if you get married someday and have children, things might be difficult for the two of you as well."

Sasha frowned. "But we get along so well, and we have God at the center of our relationship. We're not the same as his parents."

"That's true, and it's wonderful that you've found that with Brody, but that doesn't mean that he can see this clearly. I'm no psychiatrist, but he might be internalizing what his parents went through, and on some level, thinking that's what it's like for all parents, even if he knows in reality it's different for the two of you."

"That actually makes a lot of sense," Sasha said. "Maybe he just needs to understand that he and I are not doomed to fail, just because his parents had problems."

Elaine nodded. "That doesn't mean you won't have problems either. It just means that perhaps you've got a stronger foundation to start from. You'll still make mistakes," she said, "but they don't have to be the same ones Brody's parents made, or that your father and I made for that matter, and they don't have to harm your marriage."

"You and Dad had such a great marriage," Sasha said, smiling.

Elaine's heart swelled. It was a delight to have given her children the gift of a good example of marriage. "Yes, we did. But it wasn't perfect—no marriage is. And no parents are either. If you marry Brody, you will meet challenges and you will face struggles, as all married couples do. And if you have kids, you'll come across even more challenges and struggles, as all parents do. But just like your dad and me, you'll have each other, and you'll have God, and I believe with all my heart that with those things, you can build a great life together."

Sasha's eyes were full of tears, just as Elaine's were. She was glad she'd followed her intuition and asked what was going on, and she hoped she could help. What she saw between the two kids was special, and Brody was the right one for her daughter, she was certain. This was just a bump in the road, one of many to come in what she hoped would become a long, happy marriage for her dear girl.

"Thanks, Mom," Sasha said.

"Anytime, sweetie. That's what I'm here for." Elaine leaned forward and hugged her daughter tightly.

Sasha grabbed a tissue and dabbed at her eyes before glancing at her watch. "I'd better get going. I'm meeting a client early in the morning for training."

"All right. I'm so glad you're enjoying your work," Elaine said.

Sasha smiled. "Me too."

"One last thing though," Elaine said. "What did you mean in your message that you had a Skype date with a friend?"

Sasha shrugged. "It was just an old friend from the gym in Colorado who wanted to catch up. I think he may have been interested in dating me when I lived there, but I didn't feel the same way, and still don't. I guess after what Brody said, I got scared and for a brief moment, I wanted to see if maybe there could be something there with this guy. But he's not for me. I don't know what I was thinking. I love Brody, and he's the only man I'm interested in dating."

Joy blossomed in Elaine's heart, and, if she was honest, so did relief. "Don't worry. Everything will work out the way it's supposed to."

"I know, Mom. I know God has a good plan for me, and for Brody. I just really hope it's together."

"I have a feeling it will be," Elaine said.

They walked together down the stairs and headed to the front door.

"Drive safe and text me when you get home!" Elaine called out, waving as Sasha made her way out to her car.

"I will. Love you, Mom!"

"I love you too!" Elaine responded, closing the front door when Sasha began to pull out of the driveway.

She climbed the stairs and brushed her teeth and washed her face before knocking on Jan's door to say good night. Finally she settled in beneath the covers of her bed to read a devotional. Putting down the book, she closed her eyes in prayer.

"Lord," she began, "thank you so much for the blessing of my daughter. Please be with Sasha as she navigates this difficult conversation with Brody, and please give them the strength to be open about their feelings when it comes to marriage and raising a family together. Ben was such a blessing to me, and I couldn't imagine life without Jared and Sasha.

I would love to see Sasha blessed with a family of her own, if that is Your will."

Elaine continued praying a bit longer and then turned off the lamp on her bedside table, her heart lighter and filled with renewed hope for her daughter's future.

"So, you two are going back to see that photo guy?" Rose asked Jan as the two women finished loading the dishwasher just before closing time the next afternoon.

"Yep," Jan answered, taking a plate from Rose and stacking it in the machine with the others. "We're hoping they'll show something useful from that night at the gallery. We don't have anything so far and neither does law enforcement. It's a real conundrum, this one."

"You mean the great Jan and Elaine haven't figured it out in what, less than a week?" Rose teased, her blue eyes sparkling as she tossed her wheat-colored braid over her shoulder.

Jan rolled her eyes. "Four days, to be exact."

Rose chuckled. "Not that you're counting."

Jan smiled. "The clues—what few there are—just don't add up to anything. We know someone broke into the gallery and shot a hole through the wall, waking up the Leon sisters, but have no idea why," Jan said.

"And took a teddy bear too," Rose added.

"Right. If the two things are even related," Jan added.

Rose put the last cup into the dishwasher, filled the little pocket with soap, closed the lid, and shut the door. She turned on the heavy cycle before taking off her apron and throwing it over her shoulder.

"I know you and Elaine will figure it out. You always do," Rose said.

"I sure hope so. Maybe God just doesn't want us to be able to help this time, for whatever reason," Jan said.

"Somehow I don't think that's the case," Rose said, patting Jan's forearm. "I've got to run, but I'll look forward to hearing an update tomorrow."

"All right," Jan said. "Tell your dad we said hi."

Rose smiled and waved as she headed out the front door. Her father, Clifton, had shown interest in a romantic relationship with Jan some time ago, while Bob had been working in Baltimore, but it hadn't taken long for her to decide it was better if they were just friends. Jan thought he'd simply been lonely following the death of Rose's mother not too long before, and she kept praying for him. As it turned out, he seemed to have found a new companion in a new friend named Rae Burns. The very thought made Jan grin since she knew all too well how wonderful a second love could be. Bob made her happy every day.

And thinking of Bob—she'd have to ask Elaine about that dinner her cousin wanted to arrange with all the kids. It would be something to look forward to, especially if the photographs turned out to be beneficial and led to a break in the case. They'd really have something to celebrate.

"Ready?" Elaine asked, interrupting Jan's thoughts.

"Just about," Jan answered. "Let me get this wet apron off and grab my purse."

"Already ahead of you," Elaine said, grinning as she handed Jan her bag. "Here, let's trade. I'll take that apron and meet you out by my car."

"You're really eager to get to those pictures, aren't you?" Jan asked.

"I am," Elaine said, then paused. "You know, it's funny, but sometimes I have this feeling Ben is looking down from heaven, and this is his way of helping out. He did love that camera, after all."

Jan smiled at her cousin. "It's a nice thought, isn't it? I wouldn't be surprised if you're right."

A few minutes later, they were on the road to Waterville. There was some light traffic as folks commuted home from work, but nothing too bad. The afternoon light was lovely as they rode along the highway. Her heart had begun to beat faster, in anticipation of seeing the photographs, and it wasn't long before Elaine pulled her Malibu into a spot right in front of Howard's home.

The cousins rang the doorbell and were quickly invited in. Howard offered the cousins cups of tea and was as friendly as he'd been when they'd first met to drop off the film, but if she wasn't mistaken, Jan thought he might be feeling a little less cheerful than he had before.

"Is something wrong?" Jan asked finally. "Is it something to do with the photographs?"

Howard paused in the hall on the way to the living room. He turned to face Jan and Elaine. "No, no, there is nothing wrong. The photographs developed perfectly, actually."

"Oh," Elaine said as he continued leading them into his print-lined living room. "That's good news."

"It's just that…," Jan began before Elaine gave her a funny look. "Correct me if I'm wrong, but I'm getting the feeling that you're disappointed about something."

"Come, come," Howard said, giving Jan a wan smile. "Sit down."

Jan and Elaine sat on the same couch as they had before, and Jan once again looked around the room to admire the many beautiful landscape photographs, even as her stomach fluttered nervously over what he might be about to say.

Howard sat down across from them. "You see," he said, hesitating, "nothing is wrong with the quality of the photographs themselves. The negatives were in good shape, and with my equipment, I was able to make certain that they came out well, knowing how important they are to you."

"Do you mind if I ask what's bothering you then?" Jan asked, hearing the weird tone in her own voice. Elaine caught it too—there was that look again that said *what on earth is bugging you?*

"It isn't the photographs themselves," Howard explained, holding out his palms. "It's the content."

"You mean, there isn't anything concrete on them that you can see?"

His lips formed a thin line. "Not exactly," he said. "Sorry. I don't mean to sound cryptic. It's best if I just show you, but I'm afraid you'll be disappointed."

Howard got up from his chair and went over to a file cabinet in a book-filled corner of the room. Jan and Elaine, both anxious to see the pictures, exchanged a glance in the few seconds before he returned.

He stood in front of them, holding out a manila file folder, which Elaine took gently from his outstretched hand.

"Take a look," he said. "You'll see what I mean."

Slowly, Elaine removed the two photos, scanning the first one before handing it to Jan with a rueful look. Instantly, Jan's heart sank as she caught sight of the first snapshot.

"Nothing," she and Elaine said out loud simultaneously, with Jan adding. "It's just a big blur."

"That one is, yes," Howard said. "I did everything I could, but unfortunately, the raw material didn't give me much to work with." He held up his hands and chuckled apologetically.

"No," Elaine said, laughing softly, "of course it didn't. It's not your fault."

"Let's see the other," Jan said. She had to hold herself back from snatching it out of her cousin's hand. She was so eager to see it!

"I'm afraid you'll find the other just as disappointing," Howard said, tucking his hands into his pockets.

But as Elaine lifted the blurry picture and set it aside, revealing the one underneath, Jan felt a look of triumph spread across her face. She looked up to find that Elaine's expression matched her own.

"Actually," she said to Howard, "this one is far more useful."

AFTER PAYING HOWARD for developing the film and making the prints of both photos—despite his insistence that the blurry one didn't count and therefore didn't cost anything—Jan and Elaine practically ran out to the car.

"It's not really very much," Elaine said, pressing her key fob to open the doors as quickly as possible.

"Not much is still better than nothing." Jan just about jumped out of her skin to get into the car as Elaine did the same. When they were finally seated, Elaine pulled out both photos again, placing the blurry one underneath. They stared at the picture in silence, squinting as late afternoon faded into evening and the sun began its slow crawl into darkness.

"The light isn't good inside the car," Elaine said. "We should get home and take a better look there."

"We've got another clambake meeting tonight, remember? We'll be swamped with the gals not long after we get home. Let's at least check it out a little bit now. We can get a good look later."

"I'm afraid we still won't be able to see much," Jan said. "It was plenty light inside Howard's house, and we still couldn't make out too much detail in there."

"But we've still got our first clue that might actually lead us to something else," Elaine said. "And we can get Dan to have it enlarged and enhanced as soon as possible."

"Good idea," Jan agreed.

It was true: the photograph was too far away to offer much in the way of fine detail, but it was still something tangible and identifiable—an arm wearing a bracelet. The photo also bore a time stamp, confirming it was taken around the same time the Leon sisters heard the uproar in the gallery.

Jan gave a sigh, and Elaine tucked the photos back into their folder. "Who do you think it belongs to?" she asked.

"I have no idea at this point," Elaine answered. "After the clambake meeting, we can pull out the magnifying glass and see if that helps, but I'm sure we'll be able to tell more once Dan's team does their thing."

"How long do you think that will take?" Jan asked.

Elaine shook her head. "I don't know, but since the bullet hasn't yet been matched to a gun, and they haven't found out who the SUV tracks or the footprints belong to, and they don't have a license plate number, I'd say not too long. Dan will probably be as eager as we are to get a close-up so we can identify this limb."

"It has to belong to someone who was there that night, right?" Jan added. "I think it's got to be either the shooter, or the person who got shot at."

"I agree," Elaine began, "and you know what that means. If we can find the owner of this arm—"

"We find whoever who broke in," Jan finished.

CHAPTER EIGHT

Jan only just had time to set out a platter of blueberry scones before the doorbell rang—already the women were arriving for the clambake meeting. Jan stripped off her apron and headed for the front door just as Elaine walked into the east parlor, puffing a little as she carried a heavy urn of orange spice tea to put on the table between the scones and an arrangement of teacups. Even though Jan was dying to take a magnifying glass to the photos Howard had developed, it would simply have to wait.

Kate, Bianca, Kimi, Macy, and Zale shuffled inside, grabbed treats, and chatted with Jan and Elaine for a few minutes before the meeting officially began. Everyone was still in agreement about who was going to handle what, and Bianca had secured the town beach as their venue. There would be tables set up with lemonade and iced tea, as well as paper goods on the dock, and it would serve as an anchor point while the seaweed storage container and fire pit would be on the beach for everyone to gather around as the clams were cooked. The group went over a few more details and brainstormed about how to make sure everything stayed safe if the kids brought sparklers, and who would be responsible for keeping ice stocked for drinks, and by the time an hour had passed, all had been sorted out and the subject of conversation turned casual again.

"I've been meaning to ask you," Kate began, coming to help Jan gather empty cups, "how are things with Bob? I know you must be thrilled to have him back in town."

Jan's heart gave a little flutter at the mention of the man she loved. "He's been busy as ever," she said. "We talk every day, but with the clambake preparation and the break-in at the gallery, I haven't seen him in almost a week!"

"He must miss you," Kate said, her dark eyes kind.

"He does." She blushed a little. "Elaine is going to arrange a dinner with Sasha and her boyfriend soon, plus my kiddos, and Bob and I will go, along with Nathan, so I'm looking forward to that," Jan said. She found more and more that nothing gave her more enjoyment than spending time with those she loved, so she was sure the gathering would be a treat.

She and Kate chatted for a bit longer, and as Kate walked over to talk to Kimi, Jan spotted Zale, who was wearing that lovely gold bracelet Elaine had complimented her on at the gallery. Zale caught her eye and came over to say hello.

"Thanks for the blueberry scones," Zale said, lowering her voice to a whisper. "I know my mother-in-law complains about your baked goods, but we all know they truly are delicious." She winked. "And she's probably your biggest fan."

"Oh, thank you for saying so," Jan responded. It was kind of a running joke between her and Elaine. Macy could almost always find something to complain about—either the tea was too cold or it was scalding, or the pastries were too dry, but the woman had a good heart, and she showed her true feelings by sending her cottage renters to the tearoom. Jan knew their prickly friend was probably responsible for a good portion of their business.

"That is just the prettiest bracelet," Jan commented.

She reached out to get a better look at Zale's wrist, but the young woman suddenly stepped back a little, her lips forming a thin line of unease. Just then, Macy joined the two of them and must have seen the discomfort in her daughter-in-law's expression.

"Zale, is something wrong?" Macy asked.

"Oh, it's nothing," Zale said. "I've just got to run to the restroom real quick."

Macy peered at Jan, her steely eyes narrowed. "What was that all about?" she asked.

Jan's mouth was open and it took her a second to gather herself before she could respond. "I don't know," she said.

"Did you say something to offend her?" Macy asked, hands bolted to her hips.

Ignoring Macy's comment, Jan took a breath. She couldn't wait until they had that photo enlarged.

AFTER THE CLAMBAKE meeting, Bob called and Jan talked with him for a while before making herself a cup of tea and heading up to the sitting room to find Elaine. It seemed her cousin had been on the same wavelength because just as Jan entered the room, she heard Elaine say, "Okay, Nathan, sounds good. I'll see you soon," and then she hung up.

She smiled and motioned for Jan to come and sit down on the couch.

"I feel like I haven't seen Nathan in a long time," Elaine said, echoing Jan's earlier feelings about Bob.

"I know," Jan said. "We've been so busy planning the clambake and running back and forth to Waterville to get those photos developed that it has been a while for both of us, hasn't it?"

"Mmm-hmm," Elaine agreed. "We were just talking about doing that dinner with Sasha and the others, but she and I have been playing phone tag."

Jan grinned. "She's got a lot on her mind right now, what with Brody and drumming up clients."

It was true. Since moving back to Lancaster, Sasha had been busily rebuilding her personal training clientele back to the workload she'd enjoyed in Colorado.

"So far, that seems to be going well," Elaine said. "She says it's actually been easier to find people who need that kind of help here. I sometimes got the feeling there was a lot of competition back in Colorado since she was in a ski town with a big cultural focus on fitness."

"I'm glad to hear that. And the clambake planning is going smoothly." Jan said. "I think it'll be a blast to get the town together like that at the end of the summer before things quiet down, post-tourist season. I don't know why we haven't made that a tradition," Jan said. She tucked her feet up under her legs and pulled a throw over her lap, enjoying the quiet evening with her cousin. "Hey, are you ready to look at that photo?" she asked, eyeing the manila folder perched on the coffee table between them.

"Earlier I was just so eager to get to it, but with the meeting and talking to Nathan, it sort of got shuffled to the back of my mind." Elaine picked up the folder and opened it, taking out the blurry picture first. "I really wish there were something here, but I'm afraid this one's a bust," she said. She clucked her tongue with disappointment.

"Let's have a look at the good one," Jan prodded as Elaine slipped it from the folder and set it beside its blurry mate.

Elaine picked up a magnifying glass from the table and held it over the photo. The cousins studied it carefully for a moment, each silently attempting to sort out what she could see.

"Well, I can tell that's an arm with a bracelet or something very similar on it," Elaine said, squinting despite the glass. "But very little else."

"Even with the help of the magnification, it's still not much," Jan agreed. "Didn't Howard give you a thumb drive with the pictures as well?" she asked Elaine.

"Yes, it's right here in the folder," Elaine responded, retrieving a tiny, thin USB drive. "I already uploaded it and e-mailed copies to Dan—he's going to have his team enlarge and enhance them tonight, and send us a new one to print out, so we can look at it tomorrow."

"Good deal," Jan said, nodding.

"At least we've got that though, even if it isn't crystal clear," Elaine said. "It was quick thinking for whoever had the camera to try to get a picture before the person got away."

"Yeah," Jan said, "either that or it fell and the pictures snapped when the camera button hit the floor."

"That might make more sense. If there were two people in the gallery at the same time—and why else would someone have taken a shot?—then why would one of them want to leave behind evidence?" Elaine mused.

Jan shook her head. "It's still one of the weirdest cases we've helped with."

The cousins pulled away from the photo.

"I'm going to go try to catch Sasha," Elaine said, "then I'm going to bed."

"Good plan," Jan agreed. "The sooner we get to sleep, the sooner we'll get to see the picture close up."

ELAINE HADN'T SLEPT much that Thursday night, eager to see the photo enhancements Dan's team would come up with, and the next morning, she practically jumped out of bed to check her e-mail to see if he'd sent anything yet.

Sadly, no. Her phone began to ring and, thinking it was Dan, Elaine picked up and blurted out, "So have you got it yet?"

The laughter on the other end belonged to Sasha. "Well, good morning to you too, Mom," her daughter said cheerfully.

"Oh, Sasha, I'm sorry," Elaine apologized. "I was expecting a call from Dan."

"Working on another mystery, then?" Sasha asked, a hint of teasing in her tone. "Guess that's why Lancaster locals call you two the Clever Cousins."

"Oh, that's such a silly name," Elaine said, though she secretly kind of liked it. Besides, it would be hard to argue that the shoe didn't fit.

"I know, I know, but be careful investigating," Sasha said.

"Now you're starting to sound like Brian," Elaine teased. Jan's son often worried about his mother and Elaine's involvement solving crimes.

"I'm living here now, aren't I? So part of my new role is to look after you," Sasha said.

"That's very sweet," Elaine said, "but there's not much Jan and I can't handle." And it was true. She smiled to herself, thinking of all the adventures she and her cousin had experienced. It was a good thing she and Jan didn't tell their kids half of what they got up to. "Anyway," she said, changing the subject, "we've got to talk about plans."

"Right," Sasha said. "Let me just look at my calendar quick and see . . ."

"So, business is going well, I take it?" Elaine asked.

"Yes, actually. I've gotten two new clients this week and I'm starting to book out a few months, so things are looking more and more secure financially," Sasha explained. "Okay, so it looks like on my end that maybe Sunday would be good, like possibly for an after-church lunch. Or maybe dinner. Brody's available then too."

"This coming Sunday?" Elaine asked.

"Yes, that's the one," Sasha clarified.

"I'll mark that down. I'll ask Nathan if he can come along, and Jan's going to bring Bob too, plus your cousins," Elaine said, feeling the excitement build up. "We'll still need to sort out a place, or if we want to have it at the tearoom or some-one's home."

"Sounds great, Mom, but listen—I've got to run. I've got a training session in a half hour, so I'll talk to Brody about where to do a meal together and then I'll get back to you, okay?" Sasha asked, sounding slightly rushed.

"Okay, that's good with me," Elaine said, happy her daughter was busy and settling in to her new town and new apartment. "Talk soon."

"Talk soon, Mom," Sasha said. "Bye!"

"Bye, sweetie," Elaine said before hanging up her phone. She showered quickly and ran a comb through her hair, put on minimal makeup, and dressed in white capri pants and a billowy top with a colorful print of large orange hibiscus.

In talking to Sasha, she'd almost forgotten about the photo, and when she checked her e-mail again, there was a message from Dan with the enlarged and enhanced version attached.

"Jan!" Elaine called as she rushed down the steps and into the kitchen.

"What is it?" Jan responded, pouring her first cup of tea.

Elaine didn't say anything and just stood there grinning.

"You got the photo back from Dan, didn't you?" Jan asked, a similar broad smile spreading across her lips as she added a little sugar to her tea.

"I sure did," Elaine said, heading over to the office. "I'm printing it out now!" she called, opening a desk drawer to find photo paper, which she then loaded into the printer. After a few moments, several pieces of the paper were piled in the printer's tray, and Elaine gathered them up along with a roll of tape before bringing them out to the kitchen table.

"I've got to put these together. It's much bigger now and I printed it at 100 percent so we can see it as well as possible," Elaine explained as she worked.

"Why don't I grab you a cup of tea while you're doing that?" Jan offered. "It's ginger this morning."

"Thanks," Elaine said. "Just a little milk and sugar, please."

"You got it," Jan said, pulling low-fat milk from the big fridge and then adding a splash to a mug she'd retrieved from the cabinet for Elaine. She stirred in a spoonful of sugar and brought both her mug and her cousin's to the table before sitting down beside Elaine.

"All right," Elaine said as she added one last piece of tape to the back of four pieces of paper she'd put together in a square. "Here we go."

She turned it over and Jan leaned in closer as they studied it for the third time, hoping to see far more than they had before.

"Oh, it's so much easier to see now!" Jan exclaimed, folding her hands together.

"It is," Elaine agreed. "It looks like the skin is fairly tan, doesn't it?" she asked Jan.

"Yes," Jan said, narrowing her eyes. "So maybe the person spends a lot of time outdoors, or has an ethnic background with slightly darker skin. And I don't see any distinguishing marks, like freckles, scratches, or scars, do you?"

Elaine shook her head. "There aren't any tattoos either, and it's only the forearm—the person must have been wearing shorter sleeves because it's too far up the arm to see any clothing."

"Right," Jan agreed. She took a sip of her tea before bending closer. "I can see the nails here, just a bit, as the hand is bent, and I don't see any polish—at least not a color."

"True," Elaine said, "but that doesn't mean much. Most men don't have polish on, but a lot of women don't paint their nails either, so that doesn't help. Besides, I can't even tell if it's a woman's arm, or a man's."

"Obviously, the biggest clue here is that bracelet," Jan said, getting a strange look in her eyes. "I know it's possible for it to be a man's arm too, but I guess it seems a little more likely that it's a woman."

Elaine took a sip of her tea, letting the warm flavor tingle on the tip of her tongue. Jan had added just the right amounts of sugar and milk and it was delicious, making her long for the spicy flavors of the fall season that was just around the corner.

"You look like you know something I don't," Elaine said, noticing her cousin's eyes widen.

"I think I might just," Jan said. "I've seen that bracelet somewhere before."

Elaine set her tea down with a hard thud and moved closer to the photo. "You have?"

Jan nodded, biting her lip. "Yeah, actually, Zale Atherton has been wearing one lately. I saw it at the clambake meeting yesterday evening."

Suddenly, Elaine felt a surge of recognition rising from the back of her memory. "Oh my," she said, clasping a hand to her chest. "I've seen it before too. At the gallery opening," Elaine explained. She tilted her head. "You know, it's funny. She seemed a little shy about it when I complimented her on it."

Jan's blue eyes were huge. "She was the same exact way when I said something to her. It was almost as if she was uncomfortable with me mentioning it."

"What do you mean?" Elaine asked, hoping they weren't going in the direction she imagined.

"She seemed to want to avoid talking about it," Jan said, nodding slowly, in a way that made Elaine sure they were on their way to the same conclusion. "And when Macy noticed us talking about it, Zale excused herself to the bathroom."

Elaine shook her head in disbelief. "A lot of people have bracelets," she said, not wanting to jump ahead before they'd thought this out. "It could be anybody's arm wearing that one in the photo."

"Let's look again," Jan said. "Zale's bracelet was unique—it wasn't just one strand, or links—it was like the gold was twisted, almost like a pretzel that went around her wrist."

They leaned in close to peer at the picture once again.

"I hate to say it, but it does look a lot like the one Zale was wearing," Elaine said quietly. "Unfortunately, I can't see a brand name or anything like that. Dan's team did a good job, but it's still not close-up enough to see that kind of detail. I can't tell if there are any engravings either."

Jan looked away from the photo and took off her glasses to rub her eyes.

"Even if it is Zale's arm in the photo—which would be a huge jump at this point, but let's just say it is—what possible reason could she have for breaking into the gallery?" Jan asked.

"And leaving behind a bag of money," Elaine added. "I have no earthly idea."

"And, if the crimes are related," Jan said, "I can't for the life of me think of why she would want to take a little girl's teddy bear."

"It probably isn't Zale," Elaine said, hesitating, not wanting to say the next thing on her mind. "But you know we have to talk to her about it anyway."

CHAPTER NINE

After they finished studying the enlarged photograph closely, Elaine made a phone call to Dan to share their thoughts. As Jan started the baking for that Friday's customers, she listened while Elaine relayed what they'd noted about the skin color, lack of visible clothing or markings, and of course the bracelet.

Elaine hung up just as Jan put a tray of mini maple croissants into the oven, then removed her mitts to start a batch of blueberry lemon scones. Summer tourists seemed to like those, and it wouldn't be long before blueberries would go out of season, so she wanted to take advantage of the fresh fruit.

"He didn't have much to say," Elaine explained, tucking her cell phone into a pocket of her capris. "He pulled the same information from the new version of the photo."

Jan chuckled. "Wouldn't it be something if they had software that could identify a limb—a step up from facial recognition programs?"

"Yikes," Elaine said, grinning. "That might be a little too futuristic for my taste."

Jan pulled scone ingredients from the refrigerator while Elaine got out teapots and started heating water for some Earl Grey, which was a morning favorite, and a new one they had ordered recently—dragon pearls—which was a hand-rolled black tea with a deep chocolate flavor. So far, several of the more adventurous customers had tried and enjoyed it, and Jan and Elaine liked it too.

"We also know," Elaine said, "that the gun used was a Glock—Dan thought a Glock 43, probably nine millimeter—but the police don't have enough evidence from the bullet found at the scene to match it to the specific one used because there is not a gun in the evidence archive to match the bullet striations. So, unsurprisingly, the weapon's still out there with the shooter."

"That's a shame," Jan said, stirring together dry ingredients—flour, sugar, baking soda, and baking powder—into a large glass bowl as she listened to Elaine's report.

"Yes, and he said that the gunman, or gun-woman must have used gloves to load the weapon," Elaine continued.

Jan looked up. "No fingerprints on the casing, huh?"

Elaine shook her head.

Jan finished stirring the dries and started adding milk and eggs. "Why did you decide not to mention Zale's bracelet?"

"The same reason you wouldn't have," she said, and Jan knew exactly what her cousin meant.

"I didn't want to turn her into a suspect for the police before we get a chance to talk to her," Elaine finished.

"I understand," Jan said, finishing up the dough. "And you're right. I would have done the same." She returned the cold ingredients to the refrigerator and washed her hands before cleaning and flouring a space on the counter. "But you know," she said, turning over the bowl to dump out the dough, "it occurs to me that Zale does spend a lot of time outdoors."

Elaine caught her meaning quickly and paused in her task of getting out the teapots they'd use for the day. "That's true. She does all those Woodsmen competitions with Shane."

"So, even though I haven't looked at her that closely with such a thing in mind, it follows that her skin would be pretty tan most of the time from being outside in the elements a great deal," Jan said.

Elaine nodded. "Especially in the summer."

JAN AND ELAINE worked until the lunchtime lull with Rose and Archie before leaving the tearoom to visit Green Glade Cottages. Jan drove her Camry and they took Main Street down to Cottage Road, passing I Scream along the way.

"Oh!" Elaine exclaimed, licking her lips as they passed the ice cream stand. "We should text Bob and Nathan and see if they want to meet us there after we leave the cottages." Jan caught her cousin checking her expression out of the corner of her eye. "I could really use a treat after we deal with this, and summer will be over in the blink of an eye."

"Good plan," Jan agreed.

Elaine pulled out her phone and finished punching in a message to Bob and Nathan just as Jan turned onto the little road that led to the cottages' office. From the parking lot, they could see down to the dock where children were jumping off into the water, and several lawn chairs sat along the shoreline. The cottages did a booming business in the summer, and Shane and Zale helped Macy out with cleaning and running the business, and supplying firewood during the winter months.

"Ready?" Jan asked, unbuckling her seat belt.

"As I'll ever be," Elaine said.

It was hard to reconcile such a beautiful summer afternoon with the difficulty of asking a friend if she was involved in a crime involving a gunman, but it had to be done. Jan sent up a prayer asking God for the right words to talk to Zale, and for a blessing that things would turn out okay.

The cousins headed up to Macy's office, but there was a sign on the door saying she'd be back in an hour, so they glanced around until they saw a cottage a short distance up a little road that had an open door and a cart with cleaning equipment just outside.

"There," Elaine said, pointing. "They must be working on that one."

Jan nodded and they followed the dirt road to the cottage down near the water's edge. Elaine knocked on the frame of the open door and they saw Zale just inside, waving. She removed her earbuds and walked over to say hello.

"What brings you two down here?" Zale asked as Macy came out of another doorway, her brows knitting when she saw what all the commotion was about.

"Oh, we just wanted to ask you about something," Jan explained as casually as possible. Macy could be a little, well...involved.

Macy set the broom she was holding down hard on the floor, then leaned against it as she studied the cousins. "All right. Well," she said, turning to her daughter-in-law, "let me know if you need anything."

Zale smiled at her mother-in-law and motioned for Elaine and Jan to join her outside, as Macy continued to stare.

"So," she said, stuffing a rag into her pocket and wiping her hands on the apron she wore, "what's up?"

Elaine and Jan shared a glance.

"Oh, I'm so sorry," Zale apologized, tapping her forehead with the palm of her hand, "can I get you something to drink?"

"No, no, that's okay," Elaine said. "We don't want to bother you for too long."

"I should have asked before," Zale explained, wiping hair away from her face. "It's just been such a busy morning. We had several reservations end today and we're booked up back-to-back, so we've got to get the rooms cleared out right away, before the next families arrive."

"Well," Jan said, "we're glad to hear business is going well."

Zale glanced between the two of them, one corner of her mouth tipped up at their curious behavior. "What did you want to talk to me about?" she asked.

With a nod from Elaine, Jan spoke. "Don't read too much into this," she began, tentatively, "but we were just curious whether you were at the art gallery after hours the night of the exhibit opening."

Zale frowned. "Why would I have been there later that night?"

"It's nothing, we just—"

Realization suddenly spread over Zale's features, followed in quick succession by rose-colored embarrassment. "You think I was the one who broke in?"

"No, not exactly," Elaine explained weakly. "It's just that, well, one of the pieces of evidence found was a photograph." She looked at Jan.

"It's a picture of an arm," Jan explained, trying to sound as gentle as possible. "And the arm is wearing a bracelet just like the one you have on now."

Zale looked down at her wrist. "This?" she asked, confused.

Jan nodded and they were all silent for a few seconds before Macy popped her head out of the cottage.

"What in the world's going on out here?" Macy asked.

"Nothing," Zale said quickly, the rose in her skin darkening to more of a tomato shade. "Would you mind grabbing some more paper towels from the office? I think we're just about out."

Macy looked at all three of them as if they'd lost their respective minds, then shook her head and walked off in the direction of the office, presumably for more cleaning materials.

Zale watched her go, then turned back to the cousins. "Listen, the reason I've been so weird about this bracelet when you two have complimented me on it is that, last Christmas, Macy gave me a pair of earrings I didn't really care for. They were real nice, you know," she explained, her tone apologetic, "but they just weren't my style. I wore them once, so I wouldn't offend her, but then, well, I took them in and traded them for this bracelet."

"Oh," Elaine said, sounding so relieved, just the way Jan felt.

Zale continued. "She either hasn't noticed the bracelet, or doesn't care, but she hasn't asked me about it, and I decided not to mention the exchange unless she wants to know why I haven't worn the earrings." She looked from Elaine to Jan, as if needing confirmation that this was okay. "It's not lying, exactly. I just didn't want to say anything because I thought it might hurt her feelings. And I saw this bracelet when I went in to make the exchange and it was so pretty and on sale—I just had to have it. I don't usually wear jewelry, with my outdoor hobbies and all, but I fell in love with it."

"It is a nice bracelet," Jan said, taking another look at it now that they were up close.

"Shane usually gives his mom advice on what to get me for gifts anyway, so she probably wouldn't be upset if she found out. He just misjudged on the earrings and I figure there wasn't any harm in switching them out," Zale said.

"That makes sense," Elaine said, nodding.

"Also, Shane and I went out to dinner after the exhibit, and Macy was with us, and then we all came home. I've got the receipt if you'd like to see it," Zale continued.

Jan shook her head and waved a hand. "No, no, that's not necessary at all, though I would hang on to it in case Dan asks about it."

"We wanted to talk to you before he did. Like we said, we saw a similar bracelet on the arm in the photo from the crime scene, and we figured he'd come to the same conclusion soon enough and start asking around to find out if anyone's been seen wearing this bracelet. Since I'd seen it on you that day at the gallery," Elaine explained, "I thought we'd come see you. We didn't really expect that you'd broken in that night."

Zale laughed out loud. "Good," she said, "I'm glad to hear it."

Neither Jan nor Elaine mentioned the bag of money or the bear. Best keep those details to themselves rather than risk them spreading around town, since they hadn't been in any articles Jan had seen about the crime scene.

Jan turned to see Macy headed back up the dirt road, loaded down with an armful of paper towel rolls.

"We'd better get going," Elaine said quickly. "She looks irritated."

Zale grinned. "Nah, she's fine. Probably just worried about me. I'll explain everything."

"And I'm sure we'll hear about it the next time she stops in at the tearoom," Jan said, chuckling. "Have a good rest of the day, Zale, and tell Shane we said hello. We're sorry to have bugged you."

Zale waved a hand. "It's no problem. You're just crossing your t's and dotting your i's. I understand, and I'm glad this town has you to help out. I hope you catch whoever broke into the gallery. I know the Leons will feel better once you do."

Jan nodded and she and Elaine said goodbye and walked back to the car. When they were buckled in, both released audible sighs of relief.

"I'm so glad she had an explanation," Elaine said, putting words to Jan's exact feelings.

"I don't need to tell you I am too," Jan said, starting up the car. "Now, let's go get that ice cream."

"Sounds good to me," Elaine said, "but don't get too comfortable—we're not off the hook yet."

"I know," Jan said. "That's one suspect found, one suspect eliminated. But we still have to figure out how to find Uncle Cameron."

As they drove into sight of I Scream, Jan glimpsed Bob's Acura and Nathan's Cadillac sitting next to each other in the parking lot. When the cousins got out of the car, they spotted Bob and Nathan sharing a red-painted picnic table. There were several Adirondack chairs scattered across the lawn, and at the edge of the property was a koi pond surrounded by curious children and parents trying to keep them from poking their hands into the water.

Nathan and Bob stood and came over to hug Elaine and Jan.

"Where have you two been?" Bob teased, an arm still wrapped around Jan's shoulder. She looked up into his chocolate-brown eyes and smiled, admiring his handsome face framed by dark hair, silver at his temples.

"You should know better than to ask that, Bob," Nathan said, planting a kiss on top of Elaine's head. "They've probably been off solving mysteries as usual."

Bob jokingly smacked his own forehead. "Silly me," he said. "Can we get you gals some ice cream?"

"Absolutely," Elaine answered.

The two couples strolled arm in arm up to the white clapboard building decorated with buoys and lobster traps. Jan stared at the menu, taking her time in choosing as the ice cream stand would soon close up until next Memorial Day.

She put a finger to her lips, debating between lemon mousse shortbread and strawberry-pecan while Bob chatted with Charlie Picard, the owner. Charlie's faith in his product was evident in the fair-sized belly that hung over his belt, and it was impossible not to smile around the cheerful guy who liked to invent new and interesting flavors each summer. Sometimes they went over well with tourists, and sometimes not—like the basil-peach he'd once created that seemed only to find favor with Elaine.

They all ordered—vanilla for Bob, despite Jan's teasing that he could be a little more adventurous, and the new pistachio-raisin for Nathan. Elaine had chosen lemon mousse shortbread, and Jan was trying out the raspberry-almond, a choice that turned out to be just right. Bob grabbed a wad of napkins and paid for everyone's treats against much resistance from Nathan, and they made their way back to the picnic table the guys had chosen.

Silence ensued for several minutes as the four savored their ice creams and then the thick, homemade waffle cones that held them.

Nathan finished first and wiped his face and hands with a napkin. "How's everything going with the gallery break-in mystery?"

Jan licked a bit of ice cream that threatened to slip outside her cone while Elaine answered. "It's slow going, unfortunately."

"We do have a lead, though," Jan said, "so it might be slow, but it is going."

"We've got a photo that was snapped on Ben's old camera the night of the crime. It only shows a person's arm, so we're working on figuring out who the limb belongs to," Elaine explained.

"Sounds difficult," Bob said.

Jan and Elaine both nodded.

"It is," Jan said. "But we'll get through it together."

"That reminds me of something," Bob said suddenly, taking his cell phone out of his pocket. "I saw a video on Facebook this morning, from opening day at the exhibit." He unlocked the screen and began thumbing through apps. "Diane posted it."

Diane Blanchett was the owner and operator of Computer Gal, a small shop just off the main village street where everyone in town took their computers when they had problems, or when they just needed advice on all things cyber.

Jan and Elaine exchanged excited looks.

"Here it is," Bob said. He pulled up the video and set it to full screen before turning the phone so all four of them could see. "She just posted it this morning."

The caption below the video said that Diane had an aunt in the military who meant a lot to her, so she wanted to make a tangible memory of the event, rather than just visiting the exhibit. The video itself was slick and well-edited.

Along with the others, Jan leaned in close to watch. The picture spanned the crowd and featured a few short interviews with people who had lost loved ones to overseas wars, or who had family members still on active duty in foreign countries. She and Elaine had Bob replay it a couple of times, so they could study it frame by frame. There were Zale and Shane, and the Leon sisters, who talked about what inspired the exhibit, and a middle-aged woman neither of the cousins recognized as local. There was a man who was in fact wearing a gold bracelet, but whose arm was quite hairy. Jan and Elaine eliminated him quickly, sharing a little giggle over how easy it was to cross him off since the arm in the photo was fairly smooth, or at least had lighter hair. Then, as they watched a second time, Jan caught sight of Agnes Lovett, who held up an arm as she patted her hair.

"Stop the video," Elaine said, holding up a hand. "Can you go back a little, Bob?"

"Sure," he said, thumbing over the screen until the video showed the prior frames. "Is that far enough?"

"Yes," Elaine instructed. "Now, can you play it again?"

Bob nodded and he and Nathan leaned in closer to see if they could catch what Elaine was so interested in.

"Did you see that, Jan?" she asked.

Jan nodded, not even needing her cousin to explain what she'd been looking at. In the shot, Agnes's arm was tan, matching the one in the photograph, and sure enough, was adorned with a gold bracelet that looked just like the one Zale had been wearing and, more importantly, just like the one in the photo.

She and Elaine shared a glance.

"You don't think…Agnes could be the one?" Jan asked, having a hard time keeping her face from breaking into a grin.

Elaine shrugged her shoulders. "Her arm in the video matches the arm in the photograph pretty closely."

Jan rubbed the bridge of her nose. "It does."

"We'll have to talk to her," Elaine said.

"I know," Jan agreed.

They were all silent for a moment, probably thinking the same thing: could eighty-something-year-old Agnes really have broken into the gallery and shot off a gun in the early hours before dawn the night of the exhibit? Jan sure hoped not.

"You two think Agnes Lovett was involved with the crime?" Nathan asked, unable to stifle a grin.

Elaine softly punched him in the arm. "This isn't the least bit funny," she said.

"It's a *little* funny," Bob said, earning his own arm jab from Jan, who glared at him as well for good measure. "Mostly because it can't possibly be true," he added, obviously trying to get back into Jan's good graces.

Jan shook her head. "You never know," she said. "Stranger things have happened."

Elaine nodded. "We should speak with her just to cross her off the list. Then we can report to Dan that we've talked to both her and Zale. He won't believe our suspect list so far, so best to rule them out before we give it to him."

Jan agreed. All four having finished their ice cream, they chatted for a bit longer about where they might like to go to dinner this weekend, but decided that ultimately, the choice should go to Sasha and Brody. With goodbye kisses and promises to talk soon, Bob and Nathan got into their cars and Jan and Elaine piled back into the Camry to drive home.

When they arrived, the tearoom was unusually slow, so Jan let Rose go home early. The young employee was seeing a sweet guy named Brent, who had a little daughter, and Rose would soon finish culinary school, so she had plenty of things on her plate and was delighted with the extra time.

As soon as Rose dashed off, Jan put her apron on and looked around the west parlor to see who needed attending to. She smiled when she caught sight of Amber Burgess, whose eyes were closed as she bit into a fresh chocolate-almond cookie.

"Hi there again, Amber," Jan greeted. "Can I get you a refill on your tea?"

Amber smiled as she swallowed a mouthful of cookie. "Oh no, thank you," she said sweetly. "I'm almost done and I've got to get home soon."

"How's that SAT class going?" Jan asked.

Amber nodded. "It's...good. But hard. There's only about a week left, and then we all have to take the practice exam."

"Are you nervous?" Jan asked.

Amber held up a hand and tilted it back and forth. "A little," she explained, "but I think the class has been helpful and I feel much better than I would have if I hadn't taken it. I'm telling you, there are some weird words out there that I've never heard of, and probably won't ever use."

"It is strange that they put those on the test, isn't it?" Jan mused. "Most people don't use them in everyday speech."

Amber shook her head and began packing up her backpack, shoving pencils and highlighters into a pouch and tossing in a notebook while Jan took the empty cookie plate, mug, and saucer.

The teenager stood and threw the bag over one shoulder. "Thank you," she said. "I'll be back soon, I'm sure. Your desserts are just so good."

"Thank *you*," Jan said, smiling. Then, on a whim, "Since you're coming by so often, why don't we put your next visit on the house?"

Amber gave her a big grin. "You don't have to do that."

Jan shrugged. "I enjoy seeing you here, and you won't be back until next summer."

"Well, thanks," Amber said.

Jan brought Amber to the front desk and took payment for her bill, then said goodbye, smiling. She didn't know what it was about the girl—she just had such an easy-going personality for someone in the throes of high school, which seemed much rougher and more complicated now than it had when Jan had been that age, or even when her own children had. The world was tough on kids these days. If coming to the tearoom could make Amber happy for a few summer weeks, Jan would be glad to treat every now and then. She had a wonderful life herself—God had been so good to her, and she would need countless hands to add up all the blessings in her world—so spreading the joy just came naturally, and made her heart soar.

Now, she thought, returning Amber's dishes to the kitchen before she headed back into the parlor, if she could just be certain who that arm belonged to . . .

CHAPTER TEN

The next morning, Elaine called Sasha first thing but only got her daughter's voice mail. After leaving a message and making a mental note to try again later, she showered and dressed in a white cotton button-down shirt with three-quarter-inch sleeves and a skirt the color of the summer sky. She added a touch of lipstick and a pair of simple pearl earrings, then grabbed her purse and headed across the hall to see if Jan was ready yet—they were going to stop by and see if Agnes Lovett was home.

Elaine knocked on Jan's bedroom door.

"Come in," Jan said. She scanned Elaine's outfit. "Oh good, you dressed up a little too."

"Yes, I don't exactly know why," Elaine explained. "I guess I just subconsciously want Agnes to know we cared enough to do so. I know, it's strange. I just really, really am not looking forward to accusing an eighty-year-old woman of a crime."

Jan pursed her lips. "I understand, but we're not going to accuse her of anything. We're just going to talk to her. Think of it this way—she was there that day, so if it wasn't her, and I pray it wasn't, then she might know something that she can pass along to us. It might be a helpful visit, one way or the other."

"Let's hope it is," Elaine said, looking heavenward.

The two left the tearoom in Archie's capable hands, with Rose on her way shortly, and drove to Agnes's house. The octogenarian lived in a little gray Cape Cod with weathered shingle siding, blue trim, and two dormer windows upstairs. Her little garden was beautiful in the summer, with soft pink roses mixed in with green shrubbery, making her home look classically New England and just downright adorable.

A swell of dread formed in the pit of Elaine's stomach as they approached.

"It will be okay," Jan soothed.

Elaine nodded, but she felt anything but okay. "I'll just be glad when we're on the other side of it."

They knocked and waited, and Agnes opened the door slowly, beaming from the other side when she saw them.

"What a nice surprise," she greeted. "Come in, come in."

Jan and Elaine followed her. "Why don't we sit out on the back porch—the weather's so nice it'd be a shame not to get out there and enjoy it while we chat."

Elaine felt even worse at the way the sweet old woman had just invited them in without even asking what they'd come for, probably thinking they had the best of intentions. They did, really, but Agnes might not see it that way when she discovered their reason for visiting.

Agnes opened her sliding glass doors and led Jan and Elaine out to a wicker table surrounded by four chairs. The sun was shining and there was a gentle breeze to keep the air cool.

"Can I get you two anything to eat or drink?" Agnes offered.

"Oh no, thank you," Jan said. "Actually, we brought you some of our special mini maple croissants." She set the box on the table. "Please help yourself. We don't want to take up much of your time. We just came to ask you about something and then we'll get out of your hair."

"I do love those maple croissants," Agnes said, taking a seat and motioning for the cousins to do the same. "But you're not in my hair. All that's up there is Aqua Net." She tucked a palm against her tight white curls.

Elaine chuckled in spite of her nervousness. "Your hair is lovely," she complimented.

"Oh, thank you, dear," Agnes said, reaching up to pat the side of her head. "Now, what is it you wanted to ask me about?"

Elaine looked at Jan with raised eyebrows.

"We'll just jump right to it," Jan said. "We saw a video on Facebook of opening day at the Heroes of Foreign Wars exhibit at the gallery."

"Yes, yes," Agnes said, nodding.

"I'm sure you've heard or read that there was a break-in that night?" Elaine asked.

"I did hear about it," Agnes said, folding her hands in her lap. "What a terrible thing. I also heard there was a gunshot that left a hole in the art gallery wall."

"That's right," Jan said. "Agnes," she added hesitantly, "I'm afraid this will sound very strange, but we have reason to believe the person who broke in and fired that gun was wearing a gold bracelet"—she pointed to Agnes's wrist—"similar to the one you're wearing now."

Agnes looked down at her arm and her eyes went wide. "Like this one?" she asked, holding it up.

Jan and Elaine leaned closer.

"Yes," Jan said.

A strange look crossed Agnes's features and then a few seconds later, she burst out laughing. "You think *I* broke in?" Agnes pointed to her chest and then laughed some more, her eyes turning moist.

Elaine and Jan shared a nervous look.

Elaine swallowed. "No, of course not," she said. "But we don't have much to go on at this point, and when we saw you in that video and noticed that your bracelet looks like the person's who broke in, well, we knew we would have to come talk to you."

"To find out if you know or saw anything," Jan added. "We just need to be sure we're covering all our bases."

Agnes nodded, wiping her eyes. "I completely understand," she said. "Your crime-solving skills are well known around Lancaster—the Clever Cousins, I think they call you—so of course you've got to cover all your bases."

Elaine gave a wan smile. "It's not always easy, but it's always worth it," she explained. "Trust me, we wouldn't be here talking to you if we had better leads."

Agnes got up from her chair, motioning for Jan and Elaine to stay seated. She disappeared into the house and returned a moment later, holding a small piece of paper.

"Here you go," she said, handing the paper to Elaine. "I went to the gallery exhibit to see some medals that belonged to a Vietnam War veteran friend of mine. I went to the corner store early the next morning for some milk to put in my coffee. I don't always sleep well, and I woke up before dawn—old folks, you know—and realized I'd run out. I can't do without my morning cup of coffee, so . . ." She waved at the paper.

Glancing down into her hand, Elaine realized that it was a receipt. Sure enough, it placed Agnes at the store around the same time as the break-in.

"Thought I'd just make it easy for you by giving you that," Agnes said, pointing at the receipt.

Elaine handed it back. "Thank you, Agnes. We're so sorry to have bothered you."

Jan nodded.

"Oh no," Agnes said, "it's no problem at all. In fact, I think I might even be flattered that you thought I was capable of breaking in and shooting off a gun. At my age, that would be quite a feat!"

Elaine and Jan couldn't help it—they burst out laughing, and a moment later, all three women were near tears.

Finally they all quieted down and Agnes led Jan and Elaine back to the front door.

"I do have one question, though," she said. "When the gun went off, was anyone hurt?"

Jan and Elaine both shook their heads.

"We don't think so," Elaine answered, "and neither does Dan Benson."

"There wasn't any blood found inside or outside the gallery," Jan explained. "And the Leon sisters were safely ensconced upstairs the whole time."

Agnes nodded. "Well, we have that to be thankful for, don't we?"

"We sure do," Elaine agreed.

"Thanks for having us, Agnes," Jan said. "And again, we apologize for having to talk to you about this."

Agnes brushed the comment away with a hand. "It's nothing. You're just doing what you two do best, besides serving delicious tea and treats, that is, and I'm sure I'm not alone in saying I'm glad you've helped to solve so many mysteries in our little town."

Elaine smiled. "Thank you," she said.

"Anyway, why don't you two come visit me again?" Agnes added. "I'd love to see what you two think I've gotten into next."

Elaine and Jan laughed, waving as they walked back to the car.

"Whew," Jan said as soon as they heard Agnes shut her front door. "I'm glad that went as well as it did."

"She's such a peach," Elaine said, opening the driver's side door and sliding in. After buckling up while Jan did the same, Elaine paused. "You know, I'm thinking now that Cameron Lachlan might be our main suspect."

"Jessica's uncle?" Jan asked.

Elaine nodded.

Jan put a hand to her chin. "Now that I think of it, yeah, he could."

"We know he was there at the exhibit opening, and Jessica said he's been missing since then," Elaine thought out loud.

"And he has PTSD," Jan added. "So it's possible he could have somehow been involved and not even know it, if he had a flashback or something."

"Maybe we should ask Jessica more about him," Elaine said, checking her phone. "Wait—there's a voice mail here from her." She pushed the button to listen and held the phone up to her ear as Jan watched eagerly.

Her cousin must have seen Elaine's expression change to concern. "What is it?" Jan asked as Elaine put the phone down in her lap.

"It's Jessica," she said, her voice sounding startled even to her own ears. "She's at home—Dan's just left—and she wants us to come by if we can."

"Is she okay?" Jan asked, echoing her cousin's worried tone.

Elaine started the car. "I don't know," she said. "But we're going to go find out."

CHAPTER ELEVEN

Jan started to unbuckle her seat belt before Elaine even stopped the car, and as soon as they pulled up in front of Jessica's little pink house, she was out the door and up the front steps in a flash, thinking how different this visit might be from their last one. Dan's vehicle wasn't in the driveway or on the street near the curb, so he must have finished speaking to Jessica and gone already. Elaine turned off the ignition and followed quickly behind Jan.

Jessica opened the door while Jan's hand was still midair from knocking. "Oh, I'm so glad to see you two," she said. "Come in, please."

Jan noticed that Jessica had soft purple half moons beneath her eyes, and her hair was pulled into a haphazard ponytail with strands sticking out all over; she obviously hadn't been sleeping well. Hattie was playing quietly with her dollhouse when they arrived in the living room and Jessica motioned for the cousins to take a seat.

"I would offer you something to drink," Jessica said, "but I'm afraid I've only got water and milk for Hattie. I haven't had a chance to do much shopping lately."

Jan shook her head. "That's perfectly all right. We're just here to help."

Jessica nodded and released a huge breath of air. "The police have been looking for my uncle Cameron since Wednesday, when you came by to visit and we called them together."

"Have they been able to find anything helpful yet?" Elaine asked, perched on the edge of the couch. Jan could tell that her cousin was as tense as she was.

Jessica's eyes began to moisten, so Jan pulled a tissue out of the box on the coffee table and handed it to the young woman. The room filled with quiet as she dabbed at her pretty brown eyes.

Jan had the urge to go over and hug her, but they'd only met not too long ago, and she wasn't sure if that would be appropriate just yet. Still, Jessica was around the same age as her own children, and the desire to provide comfort in a time of stress was hard to resist.

"That's just the thing," Jessica said around quiet sniffling, "they have, and it's not good at all."

"What did they find?" Elaine asked, leaning forward.

Jessica glanced over at her daughter, who thankfully hadn't yet noticed that her mother was upset. "They found his truck, apparently abandoned, in the woods a few miles outside of town," she said, wiping away a tear.

"Are they certain it belongs to your uncle?" Elaine asked.

Jessica nodded, sadly. "He drives an old brown pickup—it's the only vehicle I've ever known him to have, since I was a kid. It's not a classic or anything, but they don't make that model anymore and haven't for a long time, so it's pretty distinctive. I didn't know the license plate number, but they told me they're sure it's his."

Jan glanced at Elaine. "Well, now, we don't know that anything bad has happened, dear," Jan said, hoping to offer encouragement. She couldn't bring herself to ask if law enforcement had found any blood in or around the truck, and she assumed Jessica would have mentioned something so important if they had.

"That's right," Elaine added. "It's probably a good thing. This means we know he's around town somewhere. Unless he took the bus or something, he probably hasn't gone too far."

"He doesn't like buses," Jessica said, sounding a little more hopeful. "They're too crowded. And I don't think he would try to hitch a ride with someone or anything like that."

"Gotcha," Elaine said. "Well, I'm sure the police are looking for him, but Jan and I will try our best to help you too."

"Oh, would you?" Jessica asked. "That would be too kind."

Jan waved away the young mother's comment. "Of course. Now, is there anything you can tell us that might help us figure out where he would have gone?"

Given a task, Jessica sniffed and perked up a little. "Well, his truck was located at the edge of the woods to the west of town, so he could have gone off camping like he has before. He keeps gear in his truck and likes to roam around sometimes, looking for places to set up for the night. I always told him it was dangerous and I didn't like it, but he swore he knew what he was doing. He just likes the outdoors, and I think he feels more comfortable away from too many people, and from loud noises like traffic and such. He always did love sleeping under the stars."

"That's helpful," Jan said, making mental notes about how they might begin a search.

"He's been known to have strange behavior during the long flashbacks he occasionally suffers from—sometimes for days at a time—and he always says that being in nature calms him down," Jessica continued.

"You mentioned that he keeps gear in his truck." Elaine said. "Do you think he has enough food with him to last a few days?"

Jessica nodded. "He has a bunch of those—what are they called?—MREs."

Elaine nodded. "Meals Ready to Eat," she clarified.

"Yes, those," Jessica said. "I've seen them in the backseat of his truck before. And he has a sleeping bag."

That's good, Jan thought. It could get a little chilly around there at night, but thankfully it wasn't cold enough this time of year to harm anybody.

"Jessica." Elaine wrung her hands together. "I hate to ask you this," she began, "but does your uncle keep any weapons in his truck?"

Jessica looked up from the wadded tissue in her hand. "You mean, does he have any guns?"

Elaine nodded, slowly.

"I honestly don't know," Jessica said. She pushed her shoulders up a little. "But I do know he wasn't the one who shot that hole in the wall at the art gallery." She looked between the cousins, obviously desperately wanting them to believe her.

"Are you saying you think he could have been there that night—at the gallery—but wasn't the one who stole the bear or fired a gun?" Jan asked, her mind reeling at the possibilities of what might have gone on inside that room.

Jessica shook her head. "I really, truly don't know," she said. "Oh goodness, he could be in a lot of serious trouble, couldn't he?" She looked up at Jan and Elaine, her eyes huge and sad.

"I suppose it's possible," Jan said, turning over a palm, "but let's not jump to any conclusions. The important thing now is that we find your uncle. And if we can do that before the police do, maybe we can talk to him and find out if he had anything to do with what happened that night."

Elaine murmured agreement. "If he does know something, it's possible he might actually be able to help the police. Especially if he knows what happened and who's responsible for breaking in."

"I guess he could be scared for some reason," Jessica said slowly, as if trying to reason it out, "and maybe he's hiding, wondering if he's in trouble."

Jan didn't say out loud what she was thinking—it was likely that Cameron Lachlan *was* in trouble. And he could certainly be in danger. But the main thing now was to keep Jessica's spirits up so she could provide any information that might help her uncle.

"Do you know if he has any friends around Lancaster that he might visit?" Elaine asked.

Jessica scrunched up her nose. "I don't think so. He pretty much kept to himself. I think the war changed him. As far as I know, he doesn't have any real friends."

"What about any places around here where he likes to hang out when he comes to town?" Jan asked.

"Besides the bars I've already mentioned?" Jessica asked. "I don't really know. He's gone for long walks in the woods before, and as I mentioned, I know he likes to camp out, but he hasn't ever done that when he's been here to visit us." She looked over at her daughter, who was still playing, happily unaware of the drama unfolding around her. "I don't know if he knows anything about the camping areas around here, but if he's having one of his flashbacks, he might not be in his right mind, or aware enough to make conscious choices about where he's sleeping, if he's sleeping at all."

"Does he carry a cell phone with him?" Jan asked, surprised she hadn't thought of that before. Then again, she probably could guess the answer because if he did have a phone on him, Jessica undoubtedly would have tried to contact him by now.

"No, he doesn't like them," Jessica said, confirming Jan's idea. "He never has. In some of his worst times, he even thinks the government uses them to keep track of former soldiers like himself."

Hattie wandered over to her mother and crawled into Jessica's lap. "Mama, I'm thirsty," she said.

Jessica put on a smile. "Okay, sweetie. I'm sure Mrs. Blake and Mrs. Cook are thirsty too." She winked at the cousins. "Let's go into the kitchen and get something to drink, okay?"

"Okay," Hattie said, happily jumping down and grabbing her mother's hand to lead her to the kitchen.

Jessica brought out a pitcher of cold water and poured glasses for Jan, Elaine, and herself, before getting Hattie a small glass of milk. The four sat around enjoying their beverages.

Jan noticed several photographs lined up along the part of the kitchen counter that served as a bar. Her eyes scanned the pictures before landing on one in particular that caught her attention. Jessica followed her gaze.

"That's my father, Aaron," Jessica said, a softness in her tone for the dad she'd never gotten to know.

Jan studied the picture. The young soldier, dressed in an army T-shirt, camouflage pants, and boots, was handsome. Jan could see his resemblance to his daughter in the contrast of his big, dark eyes and light hair. Looking further, she spotted something that seemed to be attached to the young soldier's belt.

"If you don't mind my asking, is that the same teddy bear as the one Hattie included in the gallery exhibit? The missing one?" Jan asked.

"Yes, the very same," Jessica said. Her features filled with unmistakable nostalgia.

Elaine chuckled warmly. "I bet the other guys in his unit gave him trouble about carrying that toy around."

Jessica giggled. "Maybe so. I wouldn't know though. From what my uncle and mom have told me, my father gave the bear to my uncle to take home to her as a gift, because she was pregnant with me, and I treasured it all throughout my childhood. I put it in a storage container in my mother's garage when I left home after high school to get a job."

Sadness shaded her eyes again.

"When Mom died of multiple sclerosis complications a couple of years later," Jessica continued, "I went back to clean out our home and I found it. Then Hattie came along, and I gave the bear to her." She was quiet for a beat. "I like to think of my dad having friends who would give him a hard time about carrying around a silly teddy bear."

After the adults finished their waters, Jessica sent Hattie off to play and walked Jan and Elaine to the door.

"It's so hard because he's an adult," Jessica explained. "He has the legal right go off on his own without telling anyone and the police don't see it as a huge deal. His home is paid off and he's retired from the military, so he doesn't have a job to report to or any major responsibilities. I'm really all he has in the world."

"But law enforcement will want to know if he was involved in the break-in," Jan said. "If they suspect him, it might actually push them to work harder to find him. I'm sure they'll send an officer or two out into the woods to search the area. Especially if they aren't able to locate him somewhere around town. In the meantime, at least you know he's probably got something to eat and a warm sleeping bag."

"We'll be praying for him," Elaine said. "And I know God will watch out for him until he turns up."

Jessica nodded.

"In the meantime," Jan added, "please keep us in the loop and don't hesitate to call or stop by the tearoom if you need anything—anything at all."

"Okay," Jessica said. "Thank you for all you've done."

"Oh, we haven't really done much," Elaine said. "We wish we had more information on the actual crime, because that might help us find your uncle, but so far all we've done is rule out a couple of unlikely suspects."

"No," Jessica said. "The fact that you care enough to check on me and to help means more than you know. I'm starting to feel far less alone in Lancaster."

She seemed to be feeling slightly better than when they'd arrived, though Jan still wished there was something more they could do besides put the word out around town and ask if anybody had seen Cameron. She was confident that Dan and his team would be able to figure out whether Jessica's uncle had a connection to the gallery break-in or not, and if he had, the police would do everything they could to locate him. In an odd way, it was actually better for Cameron if he had something to do with the break-in, especially if he turned out not to have committed any crime.

"We meant what we said about keeping in touch," Jan said. "And we'll let you know if we're able to track down any new info."

Elaine hesitated as they were saying their goodbyes at the front door. "I know you're busy," she said, "but there's a clambake coming up Labor Day weekend. Saturday, to be exact. It'll be down at the town beach—just a casual get-together for the people in Lancaster. Would you like to come?"

Jessica nodded, looking slightly uneasy.

"It'd be a great way to meet some of the townsfolk, and they would be happy to have you there," Jan added. "It's a family event, so of course Hattie would be more than welcome."

"I'll think about it," Jessica said, smiling, and Jan got the feeling that she might actually come, if not for herself, then to give Hattie a chance to make some more friends.

Jan and Elaine smiled and waved as they headed back to the Malibu.

"I really think Cameron might have had something to do with that break-in," Jan said, thinking out loud as Elaine drove home. "It can't be a coincidence that he went missing the same night the break-in occurred."

"He is retired military," Elaine said. "Maybe we can start by doing some research on his service."

Jan nodded and they drove home quietly.

Once they had closed the tearoom, made themselves dinner, and cleaned the dishes up, the cousins were both feeling very tired. Jan was glad that tomorrow was Sunday and the tearoom would be closed so there wasn't any prep work that needed to be done. She went up to her room and spent some quiet time with her Bible and journal. Just before she went to bed, she said her prayers, making sure to include Jessica and Hattie Lachlan, and she asked God to help them find Cameron, who was out there somewhere, alone and possibly unsafe, while she and Elaine spun their wheels trying to solve a case that insisted on keeping the truth at bay.

CHAPTER TWELVE

The next morning, Elaine was having a hard time follow-ing along with Pastor Mike's sermon as her thoughts spun round and round and she tried to make sense of what clues they had so far.

It was rare for her not to be able to concentrate, since their pastor's messages were always helpful and inspiring, but her mind seemed fixated on the facts of the mystery. There was the picture of the arm for starters. She and Jan had ruled out Zale Atherton and Agnes Lovett, who were the only people in town she or her cousin had seen wearing that particular sort of twisted gold bracelet, but of course that didn't mean too much. There could be any number of people who had one. In fact, she and Jan had arrived at church half an hour early since they were scheduled to be greeters that morning, and they'd taken advantage of the opportunity to look at everyone's wrists. So far, nothing new.

The bullet seemed to be a dead end, but there were still the SUV tracks and the footprints. However, as far as they knew, Dan and the police hadn't been able to match any of those yet, and they had many more resources and people to spread around looking at feet and tires than Jan and Elaine did.

And then, of course, there was Cameron Lachlan. Elaine's instincts told her his disappearance definitely had something to do with the crime, but what? After Dan had processed the evidence, she and Jan had not asked him how much money the bag held, but you could tell by looking at it that it was a lot—several thousand dollars. Yet From what Jessica had shared, her uncle did not seem overly interested in material possessions. So what would he gain from committing such a crime?

So the thing to do now was to focus on finding Cameron.

Just as the service was ending, Elaine made a mental note to call Dan to compare notes. They stood for the last hymn and she and Jan visited with the folks around their pew before heading back to the tearoom. After changing out of their church clothes, she and Jan met in the kitchen.

"What do you think we should have for lunch?" Jan asked, rummaging in the refrigerator as Elaine stood by the table, thumbing through the newspaper advertisements.

"I don't know, but something light," Elaine said as her stomach grumbled in protest. "We've got dinner tonight with Sasha and Brody and everyone, remember?"

"You're right," Jan agreed. "Don't want to fill up too much before then."

Sasha had finally decided that instead of just going out to dinner or lunch, she wanted the adults in the family to go into Waterville to go bowling. Jan had asked Brian, and he and Paula had agreed to come. Then she'd asked along Amy and Van and Tara and Jack. So Nathan was coming by with Bob to pick up Elaine and Jan, and then they would take his car to Waterville to meet Sasha and Brody, along with Jan's kids. Elaine was pleased with the choice—bowling would be more fun than just sitting down to dinner, and they'd all get a little exercise. With the case going the way it was, she could stand to work off a little nervous energy.

"How about a salad?" Jan asked, still holding a fridge door open.

"Sounds fine to me," Elaine said. "I'll put some crusty bread in the oven to go with it."

"We've got fresh kale, tomatoes, and cucumbers, and I can mix up a lemon vinaigrette," Jan suggested.

While her cousin began pulling vegetables out of the fridge to chop up, Elaine took a baguette from the pantry and sliced a few pieces to warm in the oven. She pulled butter out and set it on the table with a spreading knife.

A few minutes later, their salad ready, Jan and Elaine sat at the table. Elaine had finished looking at the weekly ads and cutting a few coupons, and had moved on to the main news section when her eye caught a headline.

"Hey, look," she said to Jan, who leaned over. "A guy named Tony Lasalle was picked up for trying to break into the Corinth Hotel."

"*Hmm,*" Jan said, not sounding too interested as she buttered a slice of bread.

"Listen to this," Elaine continued. "He insisted that the attempt to break-in was a 'misunderstanding,' and that he was really 'trying to visit an old army buddy.'"

Jan had taken a bite of her bread, but she stopped chewing and looked up. "Cameron Lachlan was in the army."

Elaine nodded. "Check this out," she said, turning the paper so Jan could look at it. "Do you notice anything interesting about the picture of Lasalle next to the article?"

Jan stared intently for a few seconds. "Oh," she said, putting down the rest of her bread. "That looks like the bracelet!"

"Yes, it does," Elaine agreed, her heart beginning a quick rhythm, "and he has a tan arm. It even seems as though he has clean, neat nails like our photo."

They looked at each other across the paper.

"Maybe it could be him!" Jan said, her tone excited. "We thought it was a woman all this time."

Elaine nodded. "It could be," she agreed, then took a bite of her salad, enjoying the juicy tomatoes and crisp cucumber slices.

"What else does the article say?" Jan asked.

Elaine swallowed. "It says the police also questioned Lasalle about the gallery break-in, but he lawyered up and refused to talk."

Jan grinned. "Are you thinking what I'm thinking?"

"Why lawyer up if he's not guilty of something?" Elaine asked, posing the rhetorical question that was on both their minds.

"Bingo!" Jan said.

ELAINE AND JAN didn't have too long to linger on their discovery of Tony Lasalle. Soon Nathan and Bob arrived to drive the four of them to Waterville. After they'd all loaded into the car, the guys were chatting up in the front seat about golf, so Elaine had an opportunity to tell Jan about the little bit of research she'd managed to do before the men arrived.

"It seems that Cameron Lachlan is pretty much a ghost—at least online," Elaine said to her cousin.

"What do you mean?" Jan asked.

"I wasn't able to find much about him aside from his rank and the years he served. I did find out that he served during the Gulf War, and that he and his brother, Aaron—Jessica's father—were in the same unit, but the information I turned up didn't say where he was stationed. And that's where it ends," Elaine explained.

"No social media or anything?" Jan asked.

Elaine heard the surprise in her cousin's voice. Even though they weren't as devoted to social media as some of the younger folks were, very few people these days had no presence at all.

"No Facebook, Twitter, nothing," Elaine clarified.

Jan scrunched up her nose. "That's too bad."

"I was hoping I could find a link between Cameron and Tony Lasalle—like maybe they served together or something—but if they did, it's not on the web for a layperson to find," Elaine said.

"We'll just have to keep looking," Jan said. "While you were still covering greeting duties this morning at church, I talked to a few people and showed them the picture Jessica e-mailed me of her uncle."

"Any leads?" Elaine asked, though she was sure Jan would have shared over lunch if she'd turned up anything important.

Sure enough, Jan shook her head. "No one knows where he is now, but a few people said they'd seen him at the gallery with Jessica and Hattie on opening day, and that he seemed a little nervous, but nothing helpful."

"We'll have to give Jessica and Dan a call tomorrow and see if anything has changed in the search for him," Elaine suggested.

Jan nodded, then got a funny look on her face. "I found something weird this morning, though, when I was checking my e-mail and browsing around."

"What?" Elaine asked, pulling out a compact mirror to freshen her lipstick before they arrived at the bowling alley.

"Well, I was looking at the reviews for the tearoom, just to see if there were any complaints or suggestions that might be useful, and there were two new reviews by the same reviewer," Jan explained.

Elaine frowned and looked at her cousin.

"Here's the strange part—one of the reviews was really, really positive, and the other was terrible," Jan continued.

"What?" Elaine asked.

Jan shrugged. "I have no idea. Makes no sense to me. One said the blueberry pie was, and I quote, the most 'capital, ostentatious, and palatial' in all of Maine, and the other said the chocolate-almond cookies were 'anhydrous, stalwart, and sinewy.'"

Elaine burst out laughing, smearing lipstick on her cheek, which caused Jan to laugh as well. "What?" she exclaimed again.

"I kid you not," Jan said.

"I don't know anyone who uses that kind of language, except maybe Archie when he's missing England," Elaine said, giggling as she pulled out a tissue to wipe away the pink streak on her skin.

"It would seem we have a very indecisive and verbose guest on our hands," Jan said.

The two were puzzled all the rest of the way to Waterville, and were still trying to figure out the weird reviews when Nathan pulled his Cadillac into the bowling alley parking lot. Elaine instantly spotted Brody's truck and rushed out of the car toward Sasha. The two kids stood outside, enjoying a summer breeze as they leaned against the vehicle. Sasha trotted over to hug her mother.

"I'm so glad to see you," Elaine said, hugging her daughter tight. She'd been thrilled when Sasha had decided to move back to Maine, and sometimes she had to pinch herself to be sure that it was real. Hugs were better than pinching though.

"Me too, Mom," Sasha said as Brody came up to her side.

"Hi there, Brody," Elaine greeted, and he gave her a hug as well.

Sasha was dressed in denim capri pants and a bright-blue tank top, while Brody wore a button-down cowboy shirt and jeans. They looked sweet together, and Elaine was happy to see her daughter so happy.

Elaine hadn't been sure of him when he and her daughter first met, and he'd even been a suspect in one of their cases involving a missing book that had once belonged to her and Jan's grandmother. But she'd since recognized what Sasha saw in the young man, and she'd grown to like him as well. She hadn't had a chance to catch up with Sasha after their recent talk, but seeing how well they were doing now made Elaine certain they'd worked through their issue.

Soon Amy and Van arrived, followed shortly by Brian and Paula, and finally Tara and Jack, who all joined Elaine, Sasha, and Brody. They said their hellos before heading inside to grab hamburgers and fries for dinner. The food arrived and Nathan had just returned to the table with sodas and water for everyone when Elaine asked Brody if he'd had a chance to stop by the Heroes of Foreign Wars exhibit.

"Yes, ma'am," Brody answered. "I have. It's a fine display."

Sasha smiled up at her boyfriend. "We went on Tuesday and looked around. It was sad but nice to see all the memorabilia."

"I'm sorry you missed seeing your dad's camera," Elaine told Sasha, who nodded.

"He loved that thing, didn't he?" Sasha commented, grinning. "He always made sure he had it whenever we went anywhere."

"He really enjoyed taking pictures of you and Jared," Elaine said. "I'm glad he did, because now I have so many."

Sasha rolled her eyes.

"When do I get to see all of them?" Brody teased.

"Never," Sasha quipped back, giving her mother a stern look. "At least not if I have anything to say about it."

Elaine laughed, enjoying their little exchange. Nathan was watching the three of them and kissed her cheek.

"What was that for?" she asked.

Her boyfriend smiled at her and she savored the loving look in his blue eyes. He was so warm and affectionate—she never had to ask how he felt about her. It had taken her a long while to move on after Ben had passed away, and at first, when Nathan's feelings had begun to seem like more than friendship, she hadn't been certain she was ready. But he'd patiently waited for her heart to change, and she was so thankful he had. God had blessed her with true love twice in a lifetime, and she didn't take it for granted, knowing some never got the chance to experience it once.

"I just like seeing you so happy," Nathan said.

Sasha smiled at the two of them and Elaine turned her attention to Brody.

"We tried a new running trail together early this morning, just outside of town," he was saying.

Sasha raised her eyebrows. "It. Was. Rough," she said.

As a fitness trainer, Elaine's daughter didn't often find herself physically challenged, but Brody, who had been an army Green Beret, enjoyed getting outdoors and keeping fit with Sasha. She had told Elaine many times that she really enjoyed the friendly, competitive challenge and the way he pushed her and made her stronger. Elaine had a feeling the two kids weren't more than a stone's throw away from deciding to spend their life together, and she was rapidly warming to the idea as well.

"But you had fun?" Jan chimed in.

Sasha nodded rapidly. "Oh yes. It was super, super hard, but also a ton of fun. It's pretty deserted, so we only saw a couple of people and a few animals."

"And how are you feeling, Amy?" Elaine asked, her eyes briefly glancing at Amy's midsection.

Amy looked at her husband, Van, with sparkling eyes and he gazed back with open adoration. Elaine knew Jan was thrilled to be on the verge of becoming a grandmother again. A person could never have too many grandkids.

"Everything's going well so far," Amy replied, resting a hand on her round stomach. "I had a little morning sickness early on, but Mom quickly reminded me that eating first thing when you get up can be a good way to combat that."

"I'm so proud of her," Van added, wrapping an arm around his wife's shoulders. "She's a trouper, and the boys are super excited about getting a new sibling. We're hoping they'll be equally excited about helping out with the baby," he said drily, causing everyone to giggle.

Jan's daughter was tall and thin, with shoulder-length blonde hair, in sharp contrast to Van's dark hair. Van was the nicest guy, and his favorite thing was to joke around and get a laugh out of anyone nearby. The couple had met when Amy went to Van's bank to apply for a loan to attend business school and Van had asked her out to dinner. Now they were happily married and parents to seven-year-old rambunctious twin boys.

"I'm just glad we were able to catch you all in one place," Jan said, grinning at her children and their significant others.

"We'd love to be around more," Tara chimed in. Jan's youngest daughter was a jewelry designer who had started her own line. Her pieces were beautiful and sold very well both online and in local stores. "But we've been so busy." She smiled at Jack Weston, her boyfriend.

"Same for us," Brian said, giving a rare grin. "It's a challenge to take time out even for a birthday."

Jan often commented that she wished her son would smile more. Even though his outward expression didn't always show it, he was a wonderful, warmhearted guy, and would do anything for the people he loved, and he adored his wife, Paula, and their kids.

Paula rolled her eyes and grinned at her husband. "Well, to be clear, we all know you aren't that thrilled about birthday attention."

Brian gently poked his wife's arm before sweetly kissing the top of her head. It was true—he'd agreed to "celebrate" on one condition: that no one bring gifts.

Paula continued, "Between the kids and our house, we've always got something going on." The couple had bought an old two-story home a few years back, but it had needed a lot of work. Since then, Paula had turned it into a lovely place, but it took time.

"It never slows down, does it?" Van commented lightheartedly. "Until it does, and you don't want it to."

They all laughed and tucked into their burgers. While they were finishing their sodas, Bob went off to purchase a few games; Nathan took advantage of his absence and took care of the dinner check. Elaine rolled her eyes, but secretly she thought it was sweet that, when they were together, the men had a friendly competition about who would cover things. Poor Brody tried to join in, but was quickly dismissed because he was "one of the kids."

Elaine wished Jared was there too, and he'd talked briefly before about moving, but it would be a challenge to move his family away from all their friends and activities, as well as to change jobs himself. Still, she could pray and dream.

When Bob came back with the receipt, they all went to the counter to rent shoes and pick out which ball to use. Then they met up at one of the lanes near the far wall, which Sasha chose because the painted slogan read, "If you don't get a strike…spare me!"

"So how are we going to divide up teams?" Jan asked, tying up her laces.

"I vote for guys against girls," Bob suggested with a wink.

"You might regret that," Brody warned, grinning. "Sasha's pretty good at just about every sport you could think of."

"How about oldies versus youngies?" Elaine chimed in, earning a look from Nathan.

"I might be decent at golf," Nathan said, "but my skill doesn't extend to bowling."

"That's okay," Bob said. "I've played a good game or two in my time."

"All right," Jan said. "Kids against us sounds good to me, but we'll have to take a pair of them to even things out. Who wants to volunteer?"

They glanced over at Sasha, Brody, Brian, Paula, Tara, Jack, and Amy and Van—no hands went up.

Bob put a hand to his chest, feigning offense. "That cuts me deep," he said, winking at Jan, who playfully shoved him in the shoulder.

Brody clapped his hands together. "How about the oldest of us join your team," he suggested, gesturing to Brian and Paula. "No offense," he added with a mischievous smile.

"Gee, thanks," Brian said, but he and Paula happily sauntered over to their side of the ball return.

With teams chosen, Sasha punched their names into the electronic scoreboard and they started up the first game. Brody went first and got a strike, which Sasha called beginner's luck, and then Jan was up next, bowling a spare, and they were on a roll.

Despite being smack in the middle of a head-scratcher of a mystery, or perhaps because of it, Elaine couldn't help but look around and feel thankful for the simple joy of seeing her loved ones playing a game together. She knew it would give her the energy and strength to do whatever they could to help Jessica find her uncle and Hattie her bear—and the police to find the art gallery invader who was still out there threatening the little town she'd grown to love so much.

CHAPTER THIRTEEN

The next morning, Jan woke nearly an hour before dawn and lay still in bed, listening to the carol of robins just outside her window. After enjoying the sweet sound for a little while, she wrapped a summer-weight robe around her shoulders, grabbed her journal and Bible, and walked out to the back porch.

The sun hadn't yet begun to rise as she sat in a chair looking out at the still, glassy surface of Chickadee Lake. A fading streak of moonlight danced across the water. Just as Jan was nearly finished with her morning prayers, she felt a large, furry being in her lap. She gave a little chuckle at God's sense of humor, and said amen before looking down into the face of Earl Grey, the tearoom's sometimes-cat.

"Good morning, boy," she said, rubbing a hand over his soft gray coat as he purred in delight. They sat together for a few moments before Jan headed inside to get ready for the day.

When Jan got to the kitchen after showering and getting dressed, she saw that Rose had already arrived and was starting to mix dough for blueberry lemon scones.

"Good morning, Rose," Jan said.

"Good morning to you too," Rose greeted in return. "These fresh blueberries are going fast and summer's almost over. I imagine this will be the next-to-last batch of these goodies until next year."

"I will miss the blueberries," Jan said, browsing in the pantry to pick out a few tea blends to feature for the day. "But then we'll have the fall flavors to look forward to—pumpkin, apple, cranberries, and the like, so I won't miss them for too long."

Rose smiled. "Isn't it wonderful how each season has something special to offer?"

Just then, Elaine came into the kitchen and joined them, grabbing a cup of the Darjeeling Jan had just finished brewing before starting toward her little office. "I've got to get the taxes done and get that check in the mail soon," she said, waving to Jan and Rose. "I should be done in an hour or so, but let me know if you need anything in the meantime."

"Thanks, but I think we two have got this," Jan said, turning back to Rose. "Archie has today off, if memory serves."

Rose nodded. "Right. He's having brunch in Augusta with Geraldine."

"Oh, how nice," Jan said. "I'm so happy for him that they found each other. They certainly have a lot of catching up to do after being apart so many years."

Geraldine Lawrence was Archie's half sister, a relationship they had only discovered not too long ago. It was a satisfying mystery for Jan and Elaine to have solved—and one of their favorites, involving a tragedy of war, a long-lost painting, and the love of a father for his two children, one of whom he had presumed dead. Since brother and sister had discovered their linked past, they spent as much time as possible getting to know each other.

"I'm glad for them too," Rose said, wiping floury hands on her apron. "I don't think Archie knew he was missing something until he found out he had a sister. Knowing Geraldine has really made him happy."

The two women spent another hour baking together, and then it was time to open the tearoom. Elaine finished preparing the taxes and joined them in serving the first crowd, which was largely made up of local regulars. Macy Atherton stopped in for a cup of ginger tea and a mini maple croissant. Despite its being "too fluffy"—Jan still wasn't certain whether Macy had meant that as a bad or a good thing—she completely devoured the treat, including the very last crumb.

Jan had to admit she was a little nervous that Macy might have found out about their inquisition into Zale's bracelet, but if she had, there was no mention of it, and Jan silently breathed a sigh of relief.

She had brought Macy's bill and the two were chatting when Jan heard someone come in through the front. She turned to see Jessica standing in the doorway, holding Hattie's little hand at her side.

"Who's that?" Macy asked, peering around Jan. "I've seen her around town, but she doesn't seem to talk to anybody."

"That's Jessica Lachlan, and she's very sweet," Jan said. "She's just busy with her job and taking care of her daughter."

"Huh," Macy said. "I'll have to go by her table on my way out and say hello."

"I'm sure she'd like that very much," Jan said, sending up a silent prayer that Macy would be extra nice to Jessica. The young mom had been through so much lately, and, as far as Jan knew, the police still hadn't been able to locate her uncle.

Jan approached Jessica and Hattie and noticed quickly that they both looked a little harried. Jessica clearly still hadn't been sleeping well, and her daughter had on a purple soccer jersey over puppy-patterned pajama pants. Every previous time Jan had seen the pair, the little girl was dressed in a cute matching outfit.

"I'm sorry to show up like this," Jessica said, her eyes full of worry. "I just didn't know where else to go."

Jan's heart filled with warm concern for the two girls, so she put an arm around Jessica's shoulder and led mother and daughter to a private corner table, ignoring Macy's curious but not unfriendly look as they passed her. Once they'd sat down, Jan offered to bring a cup of tea and a glass of milk, along with some breakfast pastries, which Jessica accepted by nodding absentmindedly.

"I'll be right back," Jan said, heading toward the kitchen without stopping to grab any empty dishes along the way. She pushed through the swinging doors and found Elaine filling a tea infuser with loose tea. Her cousin must have seen the worry in her expression.

"What's wrong?" Elaine asked, setting down the tea.

"I'm not sure yet," Jan answered, quickly filling a tray with a mug, glass, and a few croissants and scones. She poured tea into the mug from a pot that Elaine had finished with and grabbed whole milk from the fridge. "Jessica and Hattie are out there and they don't look good. Maybe you should come with me to bring out this tray."

"Uh-oh," Elaine said. "I hope she hasn't received bad news about her uncle."

"Me too," Jan said. "They look like they haven't had anything to eat this morning. They'll feel better when we get something into them, and they'll need the energy if something's wrong."

Elaine nodded and held one of the doors open for Jan, then followed her cousin out of the kitchen.

When they got back to the table, Jan could tell that feeding the two girls had been the right decision. Hattie asked nicely and then grabbed for a blueberry lemon scone. Her mother patiently spread butter on it for the little girl, then took a croissant for herself and did the same, looking slightly self-conscious about it.

"Thank you so much," Jessica said. "This is very sweet of you."

"Oh, nonsense," Jan replied. "It's on the house—don't argue. You've been through a lot lately and we're here to help."

"You're too kind," Jessica said before taking a sip of tea.

"Now," Elaine said, "tell us what happened."

Jessica's eyes shadowed like a cloudy sky before rain. "It's my uncle," she said. "They haven't found him yet."

"I'm so sorry to hear that," Jan said. Elaine nodded that she was too.

"But it's worse than that," Jessica continued. "Trooper Benson came by my house this morning—that's why we didn't have time to really get ready for the day—and he said they won't be able to continue searching for Uncle Cameron. He wants to keep the search going, but his hands are tied." Jessica looked back and forth between Jan and Elaine and her daughter, who seemed momentarily, and thankfully, to have forgotten her mother's worry as she carefully buttered a second scone the way Jessica had done for her before, then tucked into the soft pastry.

"Apparently, they haven't found any evidence that he may have been harmed, and he's an adult, so it's not illegal for him to disappear without telling anyone," Jessica explained, her voice sounding on the verge of tears.

Jan didn't say so out loud, but the fact that law enforcement hadn't discovered any indication of Cameron having been injured was a good thing. It also seemed that, even if the police had been treating him as a suspect before, they weren't now, if they'd stopped expending time and resources to look for him. But in Jan's mind, he was still a suspect, and she knew Elaine would see it the same way. The timing of his disappearance was just too close to the incident at the art gallery to be a coincidence, but they still hadn't found the connection between the two. All that was left from the crime scene was a missing bear, which, without any further knowledge, probably wouldn't seem important to the police.

But it was important to Hattie, and if Jan's instinct was correct, the bear might even be involved with Cameron's disappearance, so they needed to work fast before something happened to Jessica's uncle. He could be ill and was fending for himself, out there all alone. Someone needed to keep searching.

"The police have searched the woods near where Uncle Cameron's truck was found, but they say they can't keep sending officers to look for a guy who they think may have intentionally gone off the grid," Jessica said, her voice breaking.

Jan reached out and patted the young woman's hand. Jessica's only adult family member was missing, and as far as Jan knew, she didn't have anyone else besides Hattie. Jan thought of how she would feel if Tara were in the same situation as Jessica.

As she watched, Jessica pulled up her shoulders. "There's only one thing left to do," she said. "It's up to me to find him." She looked at Jan and Elaine. "I want to look for him but I have Hattie and I don't feel comfortable taking her out on a search."

Jan and Elaine exchanged a long look, and then Jan spoke up for both of them.

"I know you want to be the one to search for your uncle," Jan said, "but why don't you let us go out and try to find him while you stay home with Hattie?"

Jessica began shaking her head vehemently. "I can't let you do such a thing," she said. "It's way too much to ask."

"It's not," Elaine said, "and we'll be safe." She looked at Jan, who could tell her cousin had come up with a plan.

"My daughter is dating a former Green Beret, and I'm certain he'll be willing to help us look for your uncle," Elaine explained.

"What a marvelous idea!" Jan exclaimed. "He's got just the kind of training that will help us find someone who doesn't want to be found. That's perfect."

Jessica was still frowning, but after a few seconds of thinking, she seemed to be on her way to coming around. "Are you two sure about this? I could never forgive myself if you went out there to help him and something happened to either of you."

"Nothing will happen to us," Jan said. "Brody knows his stuff and we'll take every precaution. We have the time that the police don't, and we're more than willing to search for him."

It would be an adventure for a good cause, Jan thought.

After a little more convincing, Jessica finally agreed. She and her daughter finished their breakfast and Jan walked them out to their car, promising to let Jessica know as soon as they set out, and to give updates along the way.

Back inside the tearoom, the cousins told Rose what they were up to and Elaine went to her office to relay their plan to Sasha. Rose reassured them that she had things under control—it was a quiet Monday—and that she would call in Archie after his brunch if the tearoom got really busy.

Jan bused Macy's and a few other tables and put another batch of croissants in the oven. A little while later, Elaine got a phone call from her daughter and then came out of her office.

"We're good to go," Elaine said. "Brody's going to get some supplies together and come by to pick us up."

"That sounds good," Jan said. "We should probably go get changed into clothes that will work for hiking."

"Yes, we should," Elaine agreed. "And there's one more thing."

"What's that?" Jan asked as they headed toward the stairs.

"Remember at the bowling alley when Sasha was telling us about that new trail she and Brody tried?" Elaine asked.

"*Mmm-hmm,*" Jan responded, following her cousin up the steps.

"Well, Sasha said they didn't think anything of it at the time, because it's a public trail and there are campsites around the area, but she said they saw an army canteen when they veered from the trail to take in a scenic view," Elaine said.

They reached the landing and stood talking at the top of the steps. "Sasha knew about the break-in at the gallery, but I hadn't mentioned any of the case details to her. When I asked if Brody would take us out to look, though, she put two and two together and told me about the canteen."

"It might make sense to start there then, rather than go back to where his truck was found and retrace where law enforcement has already searched. If they didn't find him with dogs and all of that, it's probably because he'd moved on from that area by then," Jan said, thinking out loud.

"And Sasha and Brody's trail isn't really all that far from where his truck was—just about ten miles. If he's been out there for all this time, that's not too much ground to have covered on foot," Elaine said.

"You're right," Jan agreed.

"Brody's going to take us out there first," Elaine explained, looking at her watch. "He'll be here to meet us in about half an hour, so we'd better get ready."

The cousins headed off on different sides of the hall toward their bedrooms. Jan closed the door behind her and began rummaging through her drawers for an old long-sleeved T-shirt, and then went to her closet to pull out her grungiest pair of jeans that she generally only used for gardening.

"This'll have to do," she said out loud to herself, dressing in the closest thing she had to hiking gear.

She added thick socks and a pair of sturdy hiking boots before sitting at the edge of her bed to pray that God would protect them and keep Cameron safe until they could bring him home.

CHAPTER FOURTEEN

Elaine's heart was fluttering like dragonfly wings by the time Brody arrived in his truck, Sasha at his side, to pick up her and Jan. And as he pulled the vehicle into the parking area at Tea for Two, she realized it wasn't fear making its rhythm so fast, but rather a strong hope that their little group would find Cameron safe and sound. She said a silent prayer as Brody got out of the truck and helped the cousins into the backseat against Sasha's protest that at least one of them should sit up front.

"We're not that old yet, sweetheart," Jan said, winking at Elaine. "We can squeeze in back here just fine."

After making sure they were settled, Brody hopped in, started up the truck, and took Main Street out of town. They drove for about five minutes and then he turned and took a tree-lined road to a spot Elaine was certain she'd never been before. As they got out of the truck, Brody pulled a backpack from the bed and fixed it on, buckling its front straps across his chest.

"I've got water and food, along with stuff to make a fire in case we get lost. Cell service is a little iffy out here, but I brought a manual compass and a map of the park, so we'll be fine. No need to worry," he said in a reassuring tone.

"Oh, they're not worried," Sasha said. "Mom and Jan have been on all kinds of crazy adventures before to solve mysteries, haven't you?"

Jan laughed. "It's true, we've done some crazy things to catch bad guys and find the truth, but we do always try to be safe. The only thing that scares me about this is the chance of not coming out with Cameron Lachlan."

"If he's in here, we'll find him," Brody said with confidence. "This park isn't very big, and I've been over most of the trails. Best to start where Sasha and I saw the canteen."

"Did you pick it up when you found it?" Elaine asked as Brody walked off toward a trailhead, motioning for them to follow.

"No," he said. "It was full and we didn't want to risk taking someone's water if they were coming back for it."

"See, Brody. That's the kind of stuff you do that makes me certain you'll be a great father," Sasha whispered.

Elaine smiled to herself at what she'd overheard. Now she knew for certain that the two kids had worked through Brody's concern over becoming a dad someday, and she said a silent thank-you for an answered prayer. Her daughter had fallen for a good-hearted man. His wilderness survival skills were just an added bonus, but she prayed today that they might save Jessica's uncle.

The four had been trekking along for about half an hour and, despite wishing they were out under different circumstances, Elaine had begun to enjoy the way the summer sun felt on her back, and the quiet rhythm of her feet against the slender gravel path. The air was filled with birdsong and the warm, earthy fragrance of the season. Every now and again someone would say something and they would all get to chatting, but mostly they just walked along peacefully, savoring the nature around them as they kept their eyes open for signs of a campsite.

After about an hour, Brody suggested they stop for a break. They were taking turns drinking water when suddenly his eye caught something over Elaine's shoulder and his whole body went perfectly still.

"What is it?" she asked, an eerie feeling flooding through her.

"I think I see something, right through those trees," he said, pointing. Slowly, he set down his canteen and motioned for Jan, Elaine, and Sasha to stay where they were as he set off in the direction of whatever he'd sighted.

"What do you think it is?" Jan asked, peering after Brody into the woods.

"Who knows? He looks serious though," Sasha said just before he disappeared into the thick trees.

The three women stood in silence until Brody reappeared, motioning for them to come join him.

Hoping for good news, they walked over as quickly as possible. But when he led them to what he'd found, Elaine's heart sank.

"Oh no," she said.

It was a deserted campsite near a thin stream running with clean spring water. Elaine looked around, noting a circle of stones centering a pile of burnt-out charcoal, the flames long extinguished. There was a backpack, but no tent.

"It's full of MREs," Brody said, not bothering to explain to a former military wife what that meant. "And a few canteens full of water, just like the one Sasha and I saw on the trail when we were running Sunday morning."

Jan studied him carefully. "Do you think he's been here recently?"

Brody bent down and picked up a stick to dig through the ashes of the campfire. He shook his head. "It's hard to say. The fire's been out for a while, but that doesn't mean somebody wasn't here last night."

"How do we know if this stuff belongs to Cameron?" Elaine asked.

Brody nodded and bent to pick up the backpack. He turned it over and pointed to initials that had been embroidered onto the front pocket—*CRL*.

The backpack had to belong to him.

"But where *is* he?" Elaine asked.

"I don't know," Brody said, "but if I were hiding out and I didn't want to be found, I'd have hightailed it out of here when I heard footsteps."

"That's true," Sasha said quietly. "He could be around here somewhere and just not want us to see him."

Thinking along those lines, the four spent the next few minutes calling out to Cameron, saying that they were there to help, but it was no use.

They were just about to head back to the trail that would lead them out of the park when Elaine had an idea.

"Do you think it's okay if I look in the backpack?" she asked. "I don't want to invade someone's privacy, but if there's something in there that could help us find Cameron . . ."

"I think that would be all right under the circumstances," Jan said.

Brody nodded, so Elaine bent down next to the pack, slowly opening the front pocket. There was a pen and a couple of tattered pieces of blank paper, but nothing that would be of any help. When she opened the large compartment, though, her eyes landed on something that made her gasp.

"What is it, Mom?" Sasha asked, bending over her mother's shoulder to see inside the bag.

Elaine reached in and carefully pulled out the object.

Jan inhaled sharply. "Oh, that's Hattie's bear!"

Elaine nodded sadly, turning the stuffed toy over in her hands to examine it. "It's been torn," she said, pointing along a seam that ran the length of the bear's fabric belly.

"We have to call Dan," Jan said.

"Yes, we do," she agreed.

Elaine pulled out her cell phone, but the screen indicated that there was no service. Elaine returned the bear to the backpack and snapped a few photos before they returned to the trail and finally to Brody's truck. Once they were out in the open, she saw that her phone had two bars, so she dialed Dan's number.

"You've got to come out and see this," she said before explaining what they'd found.

Dan wasn't on duty but he patiently assured Elaine that he would send a team out right away. The four munched on granola bars and sipped water until law enforcement arrived, and then Brody led the team out to the site while Jan, Elaine, and Sasha stayed behind.

Finally they returned, and the lead officer told the group that they took photographs and would return with a canine team.

"Did you leave the backpack?" Elaine asked nervously.

The officer shook his head. "No, ma'am," he said apologetically. He explained that because Cameron was missing and his disappearance could be related to the gallery break-in, his belongings would be booked as evidence until they could locate him.

"But he'll need that food," Elaine said to Jan, Brody, and Sasha after the policeman had walked away. "What if he comes back and can't find his things?"

Brody put a hand on her shoulder. "Don't worry. He's army. He'll know what to do. He's got good training to fall back on, and, besides, we're not too far out of town. There was a convenience store on the way, remember? Unless he's hurt or something, he'd be able to make it far enough to get something to eat."

"Brody's right, Mom," Sasha said. "And that stream we saw was fresh spring water, so he's got something to drink."

Their words were comforting, but Elaine still felt terrible that Cameron Lachlan might come back to his campsite and find his backpack missing. If he was suffering a mental breakdown, something like that could make things worse for him.

"This just means we'll have to work harder to find him," Jan said to Elaine in the backseat of the truck as Brody drove them home a while later. "Let's go back to that article you saw in the paper. That Tony Lasalle character tried to break in and said he was looking for an army buddy who's staying in town—he's got to be talking about Cameron," Jan said.

"But Cameron was staying with Jessica before he ran off," Elaine said. "So why would this Lasalle guy be looking for him at the hotel?"

Jan shrugged. "Maybe he knew Cameron would be in town, but wasn't privy to where he was staying."

"Maybe Cameron didn't *want* him to know where he was staying," Elaine suggested.

"And maybe Lasalle is the reason Cameron deliberately disappeared in the first place," Jan added.

"Now we know Cameron is around here somewhere," Elaine said. "That's a good thing, and the police will start looking for him again."

"In the meantime," Jan said, "we've got to get to the Corinth and find someone who can tell us what exactly happened there, and, hopefully, why Tony might have been after Cameron."

ELAINE CAME DOWNSTAIRS the next morning to find Jan glued to the small TV they kept in the kitchen.

"What's going on?" Elaine asked, rummaging through the pantry for her espresso beans. Jan liked to tease her cousin because Elaine had developed a taste for the strong coffee during her global travels. When a mystery proved really tough, she needed what Jan called "the hard stuff" to help her sort through clues and information.

"Get a load of this," Jan said, crossing her arms and nodding toward the TV.

Elaine put the beans in the grinder and went to stand next to her cousin in front of the television.

"The reporter said that Tony Lasalle is no longer in custody," Jan explained when a commercial came on.

"What?" Elaine asked.

Jan nodded. "At least not in local police custody. He was picked up by the FBI."

Jan went quiet and the cousins turned back to the television as the commercial ended and the morning news resumed. They watched as an anchor explained that Lasalle had been picked up by the FBI when their system showed that he'd been arrested. It turned out that his alias was Allen Slayto.

"That's an anagram!" Elaine exclaimed. She ran to her office to grab a pencil and a piece of paper. Jan watched while she wrote down the letters in random order, then rearranged them to form Lasalle's name.

"Wow," Jan said, "you're right."

The anchor went on to report that Lasalle was a known criminal who mostly dealt in stolen jewels.

"And he was wearing a gold bracelet just like the one in the photo from the break-in," Elaine said, putting down her pencil. "So it's highly likely, given his criminal background, that he's the one who broke into the art gallery on opening night of the exhibit."

"Hand me that pencil and paper," Jan said, turning over the sheet when Elaine passed it to her. "So far, we know that the person who broke in was wearing a gold bracelet, and Lasalle had a matching one on in the newspaper photo from Sunday."

"Right," Elaine said. "And we know he also tried to break into the Corinth Hotel, supposedly searching for an army buddy, who could very well be Cameron."

"And Cameron went missing the night that the Heroes of Foreign Wars exhibit opened," Jan said, writing rapidly. "Also, an SUV was driving away that night after the gun went off," Jan added. "We know Cameron drives a truck, not an SUV. It's possible that Lasalle owns the SUV."

"If we can find someone who was at the Corinth the night Lasalle tried to break in, we can ask if they noticed what he was driving," Elaine suggested.

"It's crazy, isn't it?" Jan asked, tapping the pencil against the piece of notepaper. "We're pretty sure these things are all connected, but I still have no idea how or why."

"I know," Elaine said, "but at least now we've got more to go on than a photo and an innocent old lady."

Jan chuckled. "True. Though I was pretty sure all along that Agnes didn't do it."

Elaine winked at her cousin. "Never underestimate a sweet old lady," she teased. "It's the perfect cover."

"All right," Jan said. "Let's grab some breakfast and hit the road. Archie and Rose will be here soon."

"Wait a second," Elaine said, holding up a finger. "Why don't we just eat breakfast in the restaurant at the hotel? That way, we'll have an excuse for being there, and maybe we can see if we notice anybody who looks like they've been staying there for a few days. Surely some guest will have seen the commotion when Lasalle got arrested."

The ride to Waterville was lengthened by morning traffic, but Jan turned the Camry's radio to classical and they took it in stride, looking out the windows as they passed the docks on the river.

Finally, Jan pulled into the guest parking lot at the Corinth Hotel and the cousins went inside. The main lobby of the building was spacious and long, decorated with abstract art prints and boasting several seating areas peppered with modern, industrial-style furniture. A horizontal gurgling fountain full of colorful glass beads served as the lobby's centerpiece.

As they strode past the front desk, Elaine waved at a friendly concierge named Sierra, to whom she and Jan had spoken some time ago regarding a previous case.

"My stomach's getting rumbly," Elaine said.

"Mine too," Jan agreed as they entered the hotel restaurant and were greeted by a host.

Once they were seated, the cousins looked over the menu. Jan ordered orange juice and a three-cheese omelet, while Elaine opted for coffee and waffles. The food arrived shortly and they ate their breakfasts, enjoying the view of the river out the window near their table.

As they were finishing up, Elaine noticed a family of three enter the restaurant—a mother, father, and little boy. As she watched out of the corner of her eye, she noticed something helpful.

"The family that just came in," she said to Jan, "have been here for a few days."

Jan casually turned to look, giving the trio a smile as they passed her and Elaine's table. "How can you tell?" she asked.

"They had three of those little passes that they give you nowadays if you opt out of having your linens changed every day," Elaine explained.

Jan looked confused.

"Sasha told me about them. It's kind of a new practice to save on water and energy. If you don't have the housekeepers come in each day during your stay, some hotels will give you a coupon to use in the restaurant or coffee shop, by way of thanks," Elaine said.

"Smart," Jan said, nodding.

Elaine set her fork down and took a final sip of her coffee. "The father had three in his hand, probably to use on their breakfast. That means they've been here for at least three nights, and he's been saving them up."

"Good thinking," Jan said. "And good eye."

"We can thank Sasha for that one. Now, we just have to figure out a way to open up a conversation with them so we can ask if they know anything about Lasalle's attempted break-in," Elaine said.

Jan nodded to someone over Elaine's shoulder. "While I appreciate your Sherlock-level skills," she said, "why don't we just talk to the waiter instead?"

Elaine thought about this for a second and began to giggle, which started Jan giggling as well.

When the waiter arrived at the table, he smiled at both of them and said, "Mind if I ask what's so funny?"

"Oh, just something dumb," Elaine answered, setting her silverware atop her plate so that he could easily take it.

"There is something we'd like to ask you though," Jan said, handing over her orange juice glass.

"Sure, go for it," the waiter said. His name tag read Sam. He had short, curly brown hair, green eyes, and a friendly face that made it impossible to tell if he was seventeen or twenty-five.

"Did you hear anything about that attempted break-in here the other day? There was an article in Sunday's newspaper that said that a criminal named Tony Lasalle was poking around the hotel, saying he needed to find an old army buddy," Elaine explained, watching Sam's face for signs of recognition.

The waiter put a finger to his chin. "Oh yeah," he said. "I was working the late shift that night and the place was pretty quiet. I had gone out to the lobby to use my phone on a break when that happened."

Elaine saw her cousin perk up.

"Did you see or hear anything?" Jan asked, leaning toward Sam.

He shook his head. "I did, actually, but it didn't make any sense."

"That's okay. We'd like to hear it anyway," Elaine said.

Sam nodded. "The guy—Lasalle, you said—looked kind of like a mobster from an old movie or something. He was talking to the receptionist at the front desk and things got heated. He was real loud, yelling that he was looking for 'a soldier buddy' who was supposed to meet him but 'flaked out.' Now, I don't know what his problem was, but if it were me and I had made arrangements to meet someone and they didn't show, I'd just text them and see what was up," Sam said, shrugging.

"That's what most people would do," Elaine said. "It's a long shot, but did you happen to notice what he was driving when he got here?"

Sam shook his head. "No. I was just hanging out on my break. I didn't pay any attention to him until he started getting belligerent. After the receptionist tried to calm him down, she called security to escort the guy out of the building, but he ran off for the stairs. Security called the cops and they eventually caught him. He was trying to break into one of the rooms, which fortunately was empty. The cops took him into custody, so he didn't get a chance to drive away."

Jan looked at Elaine. "That means the police probably took whatever vehicle he'd come in, so it won't be here now."

"Does that help?" Sam asked, smiling, looking eager to please.

"It does, actually," Elaine said. "Thanks so much."

Sam nodded and cleared their table, and she and Jan each left a large tip on their way out.

Back in the car, the cousins went over the new information.

"Well, it's not much, but we confirmed that Lasalle has been around town looking for an army soldier," Jan said.

"And we know of an ex-soldier who's gone missing," Elaine added. "It can't be a coincidence. But I wonder if Cameron really did schedule a meeting with Lasalle, and if so, why? It doesn't sound to me like two old buddies trying to get together. Lasalle had to be steaming mad about something to get out of control like Sam described. It scared the receptionist enough to call security."

"And if Lasalle is the one who broke into the gallery, which the photo would indicate, then what was he looking for and how is that related to Cameron?" Jan mused aloud.

"And if he was the one who broke in, why would he leave behind a bag of money?" Elaine continued. "If he did hide that money under the table, maybe he came back later for it and noticed the patrol car and decided it was too risky to try to recover. It was several thousand dollars, but to a professional black market jewel dealer who is accustomed to more lucrative deals, it might not have been worth the risk."

"I still don't know," Jan said, echoing her cousin's next thought.

"So what do we do now?" Elaine asked.

They sat quietly for a few moments, thinking, before Jan started up the car.

"I think we should go see Jessica and find out if the police returned that bear to Hattie, and ask a few more questions about her uncle," Jan suggested. "Cameron Lachlan seems to be at the center of all this, and yet he's nowhere to be found, and all signs point to him wanting to keep it that way when there might be a bad guy after him."

"So what does he know that we don't?" Elaine asked, aware even as she spoke that there couldn't possibly be a simple answer.

CHAPTER FIFTEEN

When she pulled her car into Jessica's driveway later that morning, Jan had to admit to herself that she wasn't looking forward to going inside.

When they'd returned from the hike, she had left a voice mail for Jessica telling her what they'd found. She and Elaine had decided to give the young woman some space. The police would have informed her officially by now that they found Cameron's personal belongings in the woods, but that there was no sign of Cameron himself. Deep in her heart, Jan knew they should have tried to call Jessica again, but she felt terrible that they'd only discovered more bad news.

The cousins walked to the door and Jan knocked. After a few seconds, Jessica answered, looking surprisingly glad to see them.

"Come on in," she said. "I was going to call or stop by the tearoom, but Hattie and I have just been spending time together since yesterday, and sticking close to the house in case Uncle Cameron decides to come back."

"I think that's a good idea," Jan said gently, following Jessica down the hallway that had become familiar.

Jessica took the cousins to the living room and they all sat. "Hattie's upstairs playing," she said. "She's been handling this really well. I know she's not completely aware of what's going on, but she knows her mom is upset and that her great-uncle is missing, and she's being such a good girl given the stress and having the police around here."

Jessica sat stiffly in her chair, nervously wiping her hands on the worn knees of her jeans. She looked pretty, as always, but her expression revealed deep-set fatigue.

"This must be so hard on you," Elaine said. "And we're sorry that we haven't been able to find him yet."

"It's not your fault," Jessica said. "You don't owe me anything, and I'm grateful for your help. I can't thank you enough for taking this mystery under your wing."

"We know your uncle is out there," Jan said. "And we've been praying for him in addition to searching. That's just as important."

Jessica didn't look comforted, but she smiled anyway.

"There's something we wanted to ask you," Elaine began. "When we found the campsite, we took the liberty of looking inside the backpack there, just to see if we could make sure it belonged to your uncle before we called the police."

Jessica nodded, so Elaine continued. "Well, inside the bag, we found Hattie's teddy bear."

The young woman did not appear surprised. "Yes," she said, "the police brought it back to us after they decided it didn't serve as significant evidence. At this point, they're treating Uncle Cameron as a suspect in the gallery break-in, though I don't understand why." Jessica's voice faltered as she seemed to fight back tears. "He's a good man," she said. "He isn't perfect."

"No one is," Jan said softly.

"Right. But I know he wouldn't have shot off a gun inside the gallery, even if for some reason he was there that night," Jessica insisted.

Jan looked at her cousin. "I don't know if the police have said anything to you about this, but we don't think it was just Cameron."

"What do you mean?" Jessica asked, moving forward in her chair.

"We're still looking into it, but we think your uncle may have arranged a meeting with someone at the gallery that night," Jan said, being careful not to say too much. She didn't want to get Jessica's hopes up if Tony Lasalle's attempted break-in at the hotel turned out to be unrelated to the art gallery. She was certain the two events were connected, but they still needed proof.

"Oh," Jessica said, putting a hand to her chest. Her eyes darted between the cousins. "Do you think he's in big trouble with the law?" she asked.

"I'm not sure what's going on," Elaine said truthfully. "We've still got work to do to get to the bottom of this."

Jessica nodded, looking the slightest bit hopeful for the first time in a while.

"Would you mind too much if we took a look at Hattie's teddy bear?" Jan asked gently.

"Sure," Jessica said, "but I have to warn you—he's a bit of a mess right now." She got up from her chair and went over to the corner of the living room where Hattie's dollhouse and a toy box were kept. She bent down, opened the box, and then lifted out the same bear from the photograph they'd seen of Aaron Lachlan during the Gulf War.

She handed the bear to Jan, who turned it over in her hands.

The teddy bear was obviously old, and the bare patches of lost fur here and there were a testament to how well loved the toy was. However, aside from general wear from play, there was an open seam down the bear's middle, and it seemed to have lost quite a bit of stuffing.

"Was he like this before?" Elaine asked. "I mean, when you left him at the museum for the exhibit?"

Jessica shook her head. "No. He's been ratty like that for a long time, because I played with him as a child and then gave him to my daughter. The tear is new but not surprising. I've had to sew him up before."

"It must have happened while Cameron had him out in the woods," Elaine said.

"It's okay," Jessica said, waving a hand. "He's pretty worn out and this isn't the first rip he's had. I'll just sew him up again."

Jan nodded and returned the bear to Jessica.

"Do you know where your father was stationed during the Gulf War?" Elaine asked.

Jan recalled her cousin saying that the information she found online regarding Cameron had not disclosed his location overseas.

"Kuwait," Jessica answered. "He and my uncle were in the same unit." She closed her eyes briefly. "Dad was killed when his base was bombed. Cameron was there as well, but he was fortunate enough to survive, and from what my mother told me, he was the last one to see my father alive."

"Has your uncle ever talked about his time there?" Jan asked softly.

Jessica shook her head, absentmindedly rubbing the teddy bear's arm. "Not much, other than to say that my dad was thrilled to find out, just a few weeks before his death, that he was going to be a father."

Jan and Elaine shared a glance, and Jan saw her own sadness reflected in her cousin's eyes.

A few moments later, Elaine spoke. "This may sound strange," she said, "but do you know if your uncle has any friends called Tony?"

Jessica pressed her lips together and looked up at the ceiling for a few seconds. "I don't think so," she said. "As far as I know, he doesn't have buddies that he spends time with. I think he mostly keeps to himself when he's not visiting me and Hattie, but I'm not positive."

Elaine nodded.

"I sure wish I could ask him though," Jessica said sadly.

"We wish you could too," Jan said. "But please, try not to give up hope. We have every reason to believe your uncle is still out there somewhere, and we have every intention of finding him."

CHAPTER SIXTEEN

After leaving Jessica's home, Jan and Elaine decided to head to the library. Even though Elaine's previous online search of Cameron hadn't turned up any helpful information, they were still hopeful that they might be able to find something that would help them connect him to Tony Lasalle. And even though Lancaster Public Library's collection was limited, Priscilla Gates, the librarian, kept a decent periodical archive.

Jan parked her car in the library lot and she and Elaine walked inside. The library was housed in a small brick building. The circulation desk was in the center, and to its right there was a section for children. Local history and new media sections were to the left. The fiction area was upstairs, along with some nonfiction, and in the basement there were a few classrooms and a reference room. That was also where the microfiche for old newspapers and magazines was kept.

Priscilla was at the circulation desk helping a customer. "Well, hi there," she said after handing the patron a book with a slip inside. "I haven't seen either of you in a while. I've got a few new mysteries in that I know you both might want to check out."

"We've been too busy working on a real one lately to have time to read, I'm afraid," Elaine said.

Though Jan and Priscilla had hit it off right from the start, it had taken her and Elaine longer to develop a friendship, but now she really enjoyed the other woman's company, in addition to valuing her expertise and encyclopedia-like mind.

Priscilla leaned against the countertop. She was in her early forties and though she dressed conservatively and did nothing in particular to draw attention to herself, she was quite pretty, with glossy chocolate-brown hair and intelligent eyes.

"I suppose if you're here, it's because you hit a dead end," Priscilla said, raising an eyebrow.

"You suppose correctly," Elaine responded.

"It's about the break-in at the art gallery," Jan explained. "I'm sure you read about it in the newspaper, and everyone's talking about it around town."

Priscilla nodded. "They still haven't caught the person who broke in, have they?"

Elaine shook her head. "Unfortunately, no, and neither have we."

"But we're hoping to change that," Jan explained. "What have you got on Maine citizens who served in the Gulf War?"

Priscilla held up a finger. "I'll show you," she said. "Follow me."

"Why don't you two check out the local references and I'll run down to look through the newspapers?" Elaine suggested.

"Sounds like a plan," Jan said.

The two other women headed off to the left of the desk while Elaine started toward the stairs.

There was no one down in the basement, which, Elaine had to admit, made the space feel a little eerie. As she descended the last few stairs, a not unpleasant musty scent hit her—the unmistakable smell of old paper and wood. She passed the classrooms and found the reference room at the end of the hallway and opened the door. Thankfully, there was a computer filing system now, so she booted up the machine and did a search on Kuwait and the Gulf War, plus Cameron and Aaron Lachlan. She said a little prayer as she waited for the system to call up the records, and added a thank-you when it provided two references. It wasn't much, but if they were the right thing, she wouldn't need more.

She took a stubby pencil from a cup near the computer and wrote down the call numbers on a tiny slip of scrap paper, then went over to the physical archives to pull up the slides before heading to the microfiche machine. Elaine flipped on the power switch to give the machine time to warm up while she made sure that the correct lenses were in place. Then she pulled out the tray and set down the first slide, waiting for the image to appear on the screen above.

Using the buttons, she scrolled through the image until she found the pertinent article. At first, it was general, giving background on items that were missing from destroyed bomb sites. Then her eye caught something significant. The piece mentioned some soldiers from the Maine area whose quarters were located near a bombing in Kuwait, and the name of the decorated general in command—Bruce Atkins. It went on to say that he lost something valuable in the blast, but didn't say what. But the thing that stood out to Elaine was the list of soldiers stationed there—including Aaron and Cameron Lachlan.

Elaine turned the knob until the microfiche image was as clear as it could be and then printed out a paper copy. She folded it carefully before tucking it into her purse. The second call number yielded only an announcement of a memorial service from the time period for someone whose name she did not recognize.

With the piece of paper safely stowed away, Elaine put away the slides and turned off the machine, then made her way back upstairs. Once there, she put her name on a sign-in list and booted up one of the public laptops and did a search for the name of the general who had been in charge of Cameron and Aaron's division. She let out a little squeal when her search turned up an e-mail address, which she jotted down on the piece of paper that held the article.

Elaine was so engrossed in her work that she nearly jumped out of her skin when she heard a voice behind her. She turned to find Jan standing there.

"Did you find anything?" Elaine asked, her heart racing. Though she really didn't need to ask—Jan's expression contained all the answer she needed.

"No, sadly we didn't," Jan said. "Just some general information about the war and some folks from here who served.

Nothing specific, and nothing relating to Lasalle, Cameron, or Aaron."

"I didn't find anything about Lasalle either," Elaine said, and Jan's face fell.

Elaine held up a finger. "But I *did* find something about the Lachlan brothers," she said, glad to see her cousin perk up again. "They served in Kuwait together, as Jessica said, and I was able to track down the name of their commanding officer. I've got his e-mail address right here in my purse."

"Nice work!" Jan said.

"Also," Elaine continued, "I'm not sure yet what this means, but the article mentioned items missing from destroyed bomb sites, and the general who was in charge of the Lachlans' unit lost a valuable possession. Unfortunately the article didn't specify what that was. When we get home, I'm going to e-mail this general and see if he might be willing to speak to us about Cameron and Aaron."

"That is, if he's still alive," Jan said.

Elaine nodded. "The article doesn't mention his age, but you're right. Let's hope that's the case, and that he lives somewhere nearby."

"Yes. It would be nice to have a chance to talk to him in person instead of by e-mail or over the phone since we don't have much time," Jan agreed.

"Right. The sooner we can talk to him, the sooner we'll know if he has any information that might help lead us to Cameron. Then maybe we'll be able to figure out why Tony Lasalle seems to want to find him too."

ELAINE HAD E-MAILED the general the moment she and Jan got home to the tearoom on Tuesday. She checked her inbox just before she went to bed, to no avail. But she didn't sleep much at all, waking up almost every hour to check her cell phone e-mail app to see if he had written her back, as if he'd be up in the middle of the night returning messages from a person he'd never met.

Elaine finally drifted off to sleep just before dawn, only waking when the sound of her alarm grew louder and louder until Jan heard it and knocked on her door.

"Elaine!" Jan called out from the hallway. "Are you all right?"

Elaine shot up in the bed and peered at the clock, rubbing her eyes. She'd overslept. "I'm fine," she called out to her cousin. "Just missed my alarm."

"I don't see how," Jan said as she turned back towards the hallway. "That thing could wake the dead!"

Elaine chuckled and dragged herself up and out, settling her feet into her slippers as she stretched her arms over her head. Suddenly, she remembered why it had taken her so long to fall asleep in the first place, and she rushed over to grab her laptop off the bureau and bring it back to the bed. She sat, folding her legs up under her as she opened the computer and logged in to her e-mail account.

There it was! A reply from General Bruce Atkins. She grinned. Her idea of him being up late wasn't too far off except that she had it reversed—his e-mail had come that morning around four o'clock.

She read it carefully, getting excited when she saw that he'd listed his home address in Augusta and a window of time that very day when she and Jan would be welcome to stop by. She had only briefly mentioned her reason for contacting him, but had promised to explain more if they could meet in person.

Elaine slammed the laptop closed quickly, too excited to even scroll through the rest of her messages, and headed off to get ready for the day.

She had a strong inclination that this would be their last chance to find Cameron and put all the pieces together, and all she could do now was pray that it would help.

An hour later, Jan and Elaine arrived in Augusta in Elaine's Malibu. After arriving in town, they soon passed the copper capitol dome and drove along the river until they reached the general's address.

Elaine parked her car along the street and double-checked the address she'd written down that morning. "Looks like this is it," she said.

"Wow," Jan remarked, looking up at the house. "It's lovely, isn't it?"

The house was a Victorian from the early 1900s, featuring a wraparound porch, large windows, and two gables. The main portion of the home was painted tan with red detailing in select areas, and there was a screened-in porch on the back side. The cousins stood staring for a moment and Elaine wondered if Jan was feeling as nervous as she was.

"Well," Jan said, "we'd better go on in. No use standing around out here."

"I hope this works," Elaine said. "It's a long shot, but this man very well may be our last hope in solving this case."

They approached the door and rang the bell and were immediately greeted with the sound of excited barking. When the door opened, the first one to say hello was a little white-and-tan dog with long hair nearly covering his eyes.

"Well, hello there," Elaine said, and the dog did a little spin in response, his tail wagging rapidly.

A few seconds later, a woman about the cousins' age came to the door. Dressed in tan slacks and a denim button-down shirt, she was tall and attractive, with expertly styled short blonde hair and warm gray eyes. "Good morning," she said, smiling. "You must be Jan Blake and Elaine Cook."

"That's us, indeed," Elaine said.

The woman opened the door and reached out a hand in greeting, which Jan and Elaine shook in turn.

"I'm Eleanor Atkins, and this," she said, pointing to her canine friend, "is Eddie."

"So nice to meet you both," Jan said.

The woman stood back from the doorway so Jan and Elaine could enter, then led them down a long hallway toward a sitting parlor at the back of the house. The floors appeared to be hardwood throughout, and the home featured architectural details such as crown molding, pillars, and beautiful built-ins. The sitting room was painted a soft jade green, and was decorated with what seemed to be carefully chosen paintings and a few lovely sculptures. There was a fireplace surrounded by a custom bookcase, and a cream leather sofa and two chairs arranged around a central cherry coffee table.

"Please, have a seat," said Eleanor. "Would you like anything to drink? We have coffee and tea and water, of course, as well as fresh shortbread."

"Oh no, thank you," Elaine said. "We're imposing enough already this morning. There is no need to treat us as well."

Eleanor smiled and clasped her hands in front of her. "Please, I insist," she said.

Jan and Elaine shared a quick glance.

"In that case, tea would be excellent. Thank you very much," Jan said.

Eleanor nodded. "I'll go get Bruce and have those refreshments out to you right away."

It was only a moment later when a tall, handsome man with salt-and-pepper hair, dressed in pressed jeans and a short-sleeved white button-down shirt, entered the living room.

"Well, good morning, ladies," he said cheerfully. "It's so nice to have you here. As you probably have already guessed, I'm Bruce Atkins."

Jan and Elaine stood.

"Good morning, General," Elaine said. "We spoke via e-mail, and I'm so thankful you made the time to see us today."

"Please," he said, reaching out a hand to shake each of theirs, "call me Bruce. My military days are long past."

Elaine smiled, knowing that couldn't be entirely true. Having been married to a military man herself, she knew those days were never completely gone. The service got under a person's skin and became part of their very essence.

"Well, Bruce, thank you again for having us," Elaine said.

He motioned for the two women to sit first and then he took a chair across the coffee table. At that moment Eleanor arrived with a tray and served English breakfast tea to the three of them. Elaine tried a piece of shortbread and told their hostess how delicious it was.

Eleanor thanked her for the compliment and turned to leave. "I'll be in the kitchen, dear," she said to her husband. "Just let me know if you all need anything."

The general blew her a kiss and both Jan and Elaine grinned at the sweet gesture.

"You mentioned in your e-mail that you wanted to ask me about my time in Kuwait," he said to Elaine. "I know many former service members have a hard time talking about war time, but I'm somewhat of an open book. I've found over many years that talking about the difficult times can be the best way to stave off problems, so please do feel at ease to ask me anything you'd like to know."

Elaine nodded and set down the white porcelain teacup. "We're trying to help a friend whose uncle has gone missing," she explained. "He served in your division, and we're hoping you might be able to tell us a little more about him, so that we can figure out why he may have disappeared."

The general frowned. "I certainly hope he's not in harm's way," he said.

Elaine shook her head. "We have reason to believe he's probably all right, for the time being. But we want to help the police find him before that changes."

"I understand," Bruce said. "Ask away."

"The former soldier's name is Cameron Lachlan. He served with his brother, Aaron, who was killed during a bombing," Jan said.

"Ah," Bruce said, his features darkening briefly. "I consider myself very fortunate to have survived that day. God must have been watching over me when the bomb took out a portion of our base, because, sadly, I lost many men."

Elaine nodded solemnly. "I'm so sorry to hear that."

"Let me see. Aaron and Cameron were close, I recall," Bruce began. "But Aaron seemed on edge during the days before he died, as if something was bothering him. Though if that was the case, he never spoke of it to me or to anyone else I was aware of." He paused and took a sip of tea.

"We have become friends with his daughter and Cameron's niece, a young woman named Jessica," Elaine said.

The general's mouth tipped up at one corner and he set down his cup. "I had no idea that Aaron's wife was pregnant," he said, looking off into the distance. "I would very much like a chance to reach out to his daughter."

"Of course," Elaine said. "I think Jessica would appreciate that."

Bruce nodded.

"I was doing some research on Kuwait during the Gulf War, and I came across an interesting article," Elaine explained. "It mentioned that, after bombings, soldiers would sometimes come across valuables that had been lost or left behind when people fled from the blasts. Do you know anything about that?"

Something flickered across Bruce's expression that Elaine couldn't read.

"Yes, actually. It so happened that some of the places that were destroyed housed very wealthy people, and on occasion, jewels and such would be uncovered in the rubble. As far as I know, that wasn't the case where we were," he said.

"Oh," Elaine said. She had to admit she'd hoped there would be some thread between what was mentioned in that article and what had happened at the art gallery. She wasn't sure what or how, but it was there in the back of her mind—she just needed more information.

"However," he said, and both Jan and Elaine looked up eagerly. "I did lose something quite valuable myself during an enemy attack, though not the one that took Aaron. This one was about a week before that."

Elaine nodded for him to go on.

"You see, my lovely wife, Eleanor—whom you met—came from a very wealthy southern family. When she turned eighteen, her mother gave her a diamond—a family heirloom—that had belonged to them for hundreds of years, dating all the way back to the 1700s when her people were a clan in Scotland," Bruce said.

Elaine felt herself leaning forward in her seat.

"Ellie usually wore the diamond on a necklace. She said it had always brought the women in her family good fortune." He grinned. "Now, I'm not a man who believes in such things. I believe God has a plan for each of us and He carries it out as He wills, but it was important to her that I take it with me when I went off to war. Ellie insisted she couldn't let me go without it, and I'm not one to tell my wife no. I would do just about anything to make her happy."

Elaine and Jan looked at each other and smiled.

"So, I had her put it on a more masculine chain, and I wore it every day," Bruce said, smiling softly, "but unfortunately, I lost it during that particular blast. And as far as I know, it was not found in the rubble that remained. I went back and looked for it when I had a chance."

Elaine's pulse began to race as she wrapped her mind around this new information.

"My wife forgave me when I returned home. She said she was just glad to have me back safe, but I know that gem meant a lot to her, and she would have liked to have passed it along to our daughter. That is—if Ellie and I had ever been blessed with children" he said, a lifetime of memory clouding his features. "But that's just my story. I don't see how it could possibly help you, so I apologize if I've wasted your time. I would like to be able to tell you more about the Lachlan brothers, but they were so close—more friends than brothers—that they didn't share much of themselves with others. They got along well with the men, and they never caused trouble, but they were sort of an insular unit, if that makes sense."

"It does," Elaine said. "And it would be a long story to explain how, but I think you may have helped us more than you know."

The general smiled and put his hands together. "I'm glad. And I meant what I said earlier. I don't have much to share with Aaron's daughter, but I can tell her that her father was a kind man, and that he loved his wife—her mother—dearly.

As I said, I didn't know she was pregnant, but I know he would have been looking forward to a child very much. And it may explain some of his behavior toward the end, or at least why he seemed to walk around carrying more weight on his shoulders than usual, as if he was worried. It can't be easy to know a baby is coming when you're away at war."

"No, it can't," Elaine agreed, knowing all too well what that experience was like for military fathers.

"We're so thankful for your time," Jan said, standing slowly as Elaine followed.

"It was a pleasure talking with you," Bruce said. "And Elaine, you have my e-mail. If Aaron's daughter would like to hear from me, you're very welcome to pass it along to her."

"I'll do that," Elaine said, reaching out for Bruce's hand.

He took it in one of his own and patted it warmly with his other. "I wish her the very best," he said.

The cousins left the house a few moments later, thanking Eleanor again on their way out for the delicious treats. Elaine almost bounded out to the car, excited to share with Jan what she had been piecing together as the general spoke.

CHAPTER SEVENTEEN

Elaine was inside the car with it running by the time Jan caught up with her. "What have you got up your sleeve?" Jan asked as she climbed inside. She could tell her cousin had been cooking up something as Bruce Atkins was telling his story, but she didn't know what.

"Remember that article I told you about on the way home from the library?" Elaine asked as she pulled out into the street.

Jan nodded as her cousin drove through town and merged onto I-95, which would take them back to Lancaster.

"It was about the looting that sometimes took place after bombings or attacks. Apparently, that's not uncommon during war, and sometimes soldiers—on both sides—help themselves to whatever they can find," Elaine explained, her eyes on the road.

She heard Jan's sharp intake of breath. "You're wondering if maybe someone else found that diamond."

"Right," Elaine said. "And maybe, just maybe, that person wanted to hide it in a place where no one else would have a chance of finding it."

"Oh my goodness," Jan said.

Out of the corner of her eye, Elaine saw a hand fly to her cousin's mouth, and she knew Jan was tracking along the lines she'd already thought through.

"Do you remember what Jessica said yesterday when we were looking at that tear along the seam of Hattie's bear? About having had to sew it up before?" Elaine asked.

"Yes, I do," Jan answered, clapping her hands together. "And that piece on the news that mentioned Tony Lasalle, also known as Allen Slayto, is a known jewel thief!"

"Exactly," Elaine said, a grin spreading across her face as she steered the car along the highway. "Aaron and Cameron were in the same division under the general, who lost the valuable diamond his wife gave him."

"And the bear was torn up after Cameron took it, as if someone was looking inside it for something," Jan added.

"I'm not positive just yet," Elaine continued, "but I'm thinking this has to have something to do with the break-in at the art gallery, and the money that was left." She glanced quickly over at her cousin, her mind swimming as the puzzle pieces finally began to interlock.

"So it's very possible that someone could have hidden a jewel—the diamond—inside of Hattie's bear," Jan said.

Elaine nodded.

"But I still don't understand how Cameron is involved, or how Lasalle learned about the jewel," Jan added.

TWENTY MINUTES LATER, having talked over her idea with Jan, Elaine parked her red car across the street from Jessica

Lachlan's home. There was a truck sitting out front at the curb. She and Jan took a moment to collect themselves and then headed to the door.

Elaine couldn't speak for her cousin, but her own heartbeat was racing along at a rabbit's pace as she knocked a few times, a little too loudly. Her knock was answered by the sound of little feet pattering down the stairs and then the door swung open and Hattie's sweet face appeared.

"Hiya," said the little girl.

"Hi, doll, how are you doing?" Jan greeted. "Can we talk to your mother, please?"

Hattie nodded. She was wearing a pink princess dress with that favorite soccer jersey of hers on top. Elaine could see the puffy taffeta sleeves poking out, and she had a plastic tiara on her head with a big diamond glued to the front.

Elaine's eyes grew wide as saucers when she caught sight of the gleaming jewel, and she felt her neck grow warm as she elbowed Jan in her cousin's side.

Jan looked at Elaine as if to ask *what*, but Elaine pointed her eyes in the direction of the child's headpiece and then Jan gasped as she understood.

"What's wrong?" Hattie asked, tilting her head and crossing her arms. "Do you like my pretty tiara?" She did a little twirl, her skirt spinning out around her.

Elaine nearly choked. "Yes, sweetie," she said, her voice coming out high-pitched, "it's beautiful."

Finally Jessica came up behind her daughter and Elaine tried to steady her breath so she could speak like a normal person.

"Hi, Jan, Elaine," Jessica said, sounding more at ease than they'd seen her lately. She looked like she was about to invite them in, but hesitated.

Jan and Elaine said hello and stood there awkwardly for a beat before Elaine asked, "Do you mind if we come in for a moment?"

Jessica looked nervously behind her into the house. "Um, I'm not sure now's a good time," she said, her expression apologetic.

Jan and Elaine shared a knowing glance, and it suddenly hit Elaine—the brown truck parked at the curb.

"We have some very important news to share," Jan said.

Jessica looked over her shoulder again as her daughter began to wiggle. "Just give me one moment," she said, holding up a pointer finger. She started to turn into the house.

"Jessica!" Elaine called out, giving the young woman pause. "We know he's here."

Jessica stopped and was still for several seconds. "You do?" she asked, her features betraying the anxiety and guilt she must have felt.

The cousins nodded.

"But we also think we figured out what might have happened, and we'd like a chance to talk to you about it. We're hoping your uncle will have some insight as well," Elaine continued.

A plethora of emotions warred across Jessica's pretty face, but finally she gave them a single nod. "Come in," she said, hanging her head as she stepped aside in the doorway. "But please, don't call the police...at least not yet," Jessica added sadly.

Elaine nodded. She didn't plan to call them at all. She hoped that, once they'd spoken to him, Cameron would find the will to do so himself.

There was a different feel inside as they entered the home, as if some of its life had been brought back.

Jessica led them into the living room, Hattie following close behind her mother as she paused to call out upstairs, "It's okay, Uncle Cam. You can come down."

Following Jessica's lead, Jan and Elaine sat down on the living room couch which had become so familiar of late. They waited a moment and then a man came into the room.

As she looked up, Elaine saw him and felt a tug at her heart. Cameron Lachlan was wire-thin with hair that needed a trim, and a scraggly beard. He wore an old gray hole-ridden army workout T-shirt and camouflage cargo pants, along with combat boots and an unmistakably guilty expression. His chin down, he peered at the cousins with eyes the same exact color as his niece's.

"Hello," Cameron said, his hands hanging at his sides as if he wasn't quite sure what to do with them.

"Hi, Cameron," Jan said gently. "It's nice to finally meet you. I'm Jan, and this is my cousin Elaine."

Cameron hesitated before coming closer, and tentatively reached out a hand, which Elaine took in her own.

"You already know this, but I'm Cameron Lachlan, Jessica's uncle and Hattie's great-uncle," he said softly, offering a wary smile.

"Yes, we've heard a lot about you," Elaine said. "And we'd like to share about that and hopefully hear more, if that's okay with you?"

Cameron looked at Jessica, who gave him an encouraging nod.

"It's taken us a while to figure this out," Elaine began, "but we believe that there was a diamond hidden inside Hattie's teddy bear, and that someone found out about it, and took that bear from the Heroes of Foreign Wars exhibit."

Cameron's features didn't give any indication of what he might be thinking, so Elaine continued.

"And we think that maybe another person, possibly Tony Lasalle, a jewel thief known to the FBI, showed up at the gallery with money—which was left behind after the break-in—to purchase the diamond from the person who found it inside of the bear." Elaine looked at Jan. "Beyond that, though, we're having some trouble connecting the dots."

"We don't understand why money was left behind, and why a gunshot went off the night of the break-in," Jan added.

Cameron was perfectly still for a long moment, then finally he nodded his head. "You're mighty smart women," he said, raising his eyebrows and issuing a wan grin. "This is a long story, but if you've figured out all you have so far, it seems you deserve to hear it."

Cameron looked at his niece again.

"Go ahead," Jessica said. "But first come and sit down." She patted the arm of the chair next to hers and he did as she suggested.

"Do you know about the bombing and the diamond?" he asked, and the cousins nodded.

"Well, my brother and I were serving together in Kuwait at the time, and there was an air raid," Cameron started. "Aaron was…was badly hurt."

He paused and Elaine looked down into her hands, feeling the emotions of this stranger she'd never met but knew so much about.

"When my brother realized he would not survive the explosion, he gave me that teddy bear," Cameron said, pointing towards a corner of the living room.

Elaine's eyes followed his gesture and landed on the stuffed toy that now belonged to Hattie; the seam along its belly had been carefully sewn back together.

"He wanted me to pass the bear along to his wife—Jessica's mother—who was pregnant with Jess at the time. Aaron had just found out in a letter about two weeks before, and somewhere along the way he bought that bear and had attached it to his belt. He carried it around for several days."

Cameron took in a deep breath and Jessica passed him a glass of water from a nearby end table.

"I didn't find out until later that my brother had hidden a large diamond inside the bear. I imagine he found it among the battle rubble—there'd been another bomb the week before. After I got home, I gave the bear to Jessica's mom, and

I looked after the pair until she died." He looked fondly over at his niece and grandniece.

Jessica picked Hattie up and placed the child on her knee, wrapping her arms around the girl's little waist.

"I kept in touch with Jess, visited often, and when Hattie was born and her no-good father didn't stick around to raise her, I came by more and more," he explained. "I wanted them to have a father and grandfather figure in their lives."

Elaine could hear the tender care in his voice and see it on his face as he looked at the two girls who made up his family.

"After I'd spent years seeing the photos Aaron had sent in the mail to his wife—a couple of them showing him carrying the bear on his belt, which the other guys and I teased him about a lot, a buddy of mine sent me an article that talked about missing items from the war," Cameron said.

Elaine nodded.

"I started to wonder if there was a reason my little brother had been carrying that bear around on his belt instead of leaving it with his other gear. I decided to find out the next time I visited the girls, and sure enough, when I felt the bear, there was a small, hard knot in its middle."

Jan and Elaine shared a glance, understanding that their theory had been correct.

"I'm not proud to say this, but I ripped it open one night when I was visiting and Jessica and Hattie were asleep."

He looked over at his niece, with whom he'd obviously shared this story when he'd returned to her house. There was no surprise in her expression.

"When I opened it up, I found the diamond, then sewed it back up, leaving the jewel inside," he said. "I wanted to tell Jess, but I thought it would be safer if she didn't know about it. I knew she struggled sometimes to make ends meet, and that Hattie might want to go to college someday."

"So you came up with a plan to sell the diamond?" Elaine asked.

Cameron's nod confirmed her conclusion. "I talked to some not-so-savory folks, and I found a guy—Lasalle—who said he wanted to buy it and offered what I had researched was a fair price. The gem isn't as high-value as the merchandise he usually deals with, but he must have believed he could sell it for a higher price than I was asking."

"So you set up a meeting with Lasalle?" Jan asked.

"Yes. I didn't want to take the bear from Hattie," Cameron explained. "She's so attached to it and she sleeps with it at night. But I thought the long-term benefits would outweigh the short-term sadness, so I convinced Jess to have her put the bear in the Heroes exhibit just for the first day. Then when she was supposed to bring the bear home, I created a little distraction so that it got left behind at the gallery."

"And Lasalle agreed to meet you there the night of the opening, after the gallery had closed," Elaine said. "And he brought the money in exchange for the gem that was inside the bear."

Cameron nodded. "I figured I'd bring the bear back to Hattie later that night, after I sold the diamond in its belly."

Jessica shook her head sadly. "I had no idea he was up to something so dangerous," she said, "or I would have found a way to stop him."

Cameron's features registered shame. "I picked the lock on the gallery door and let myself in before Lasalle was set to arrive. But when I opened up the bear, I was shocked to find that there was nothing inside."

"Hattie had accidentally torn the bear recently," Jessica chimed in. "I'm always having to sew him up."

"And you didn't know she'd found the jewel and taken it out," Elaine said as everything slid into place in her mind.

"I found it in her play jewelry box," Jessica said, "but I had no idea it was valuable."

All four pairs of adult eyes shot to Hattie's tiara.

"Until now," Jessica added. "Hattie asked me a while back to glue it onto the front of her tiara, so I did." The young woman looked stunned as she put a hand over her mouth.

Cameron looked back at Jan and Elaine. "When Lasalle found out I had nothing to sell, needless to say, he was angry. There was a brawl, and he fired a warning shot, but I was able to get away from him. Then we heard noise upstairs and saw a light go on and he scrammed. He's got a lengthy criminal history, so it wouldn't take much to put him away for a long time if the police had evidence to pin something on him. I wouldn't be surprised if he weighed the time in jail against the bag of money he'd dropped and chose to leave it in order to have ample time to escape. It's likely he snuck back to the gallery to retrieve the money, but by then the police had a regular patrol car assigned. He probably thought I grabbed the money before I got out, which is why he came looking for me at the hotel."

Elaine turned to Jan. "Ben's camera must have been knocked off the table and taken the photographs during the scuffle."

"And the noise from the scuffle is what first woke the Leon sisters," Jan added.

"Then Lasalle drove off in his black SUV," Cameron concluded.

They were all quiet for a moment as the full story sunk in.

"Why did you disappear after that, Cameron?" Elaine asked gently.

Cameron shared a glance with Jessica. "I was pretty sure Lasalle would come after me—like I said, it's possible he thought I'd taken the money—and I found out later that he had when I saw a news story about him trying to break into the Corinth. I guess he knew I wasn't from around here and probably meant to check all the local hotels. I didn't want to put Jess and Hattie in danger."

"We found your campsite with the teddy bear, and figured you'd been hiding in the woods," Jan said.

Cameron nodded. "I'm so sorry I didn't tell you a long time ago, Jessica," he said, turning to face his niece. "And sorry that I ran off like that."

"You just wanted to help them financially, didn't you?" Elaine asked.

Cameron looked at her remorsefully. "I should have found another way, but I didn't know who the jewel belonged to and

I didn't have a clue how to get it back to whoever owned it before. And I thought if I tried to sell it to a reputable buyer, they would think I was a thief."

"You didn't know that the general had lost his diamond?" Jan asked.

Cameron looked confused. "General Atkins? The jewel was his?"

Elaine nodded. "We think so. We spoke to him just this morning and he told us about how he'd lost it in the bombing the week before Aaron was killed. About the time Aaron started wearing the bear on his belt."

"I didn't know," Cameron said, sounding a little dazed. "If I had, I would have given it back to him."

Something in his voice assured Elaine that he was being honest.

Cameron rubbed his face with both hands before speaking. "Look, I know it might be hard to believe, but I know that my brother wouldn't have taken it either if he'd known it belonged to the general," he said firmly. "We respected the guy, and Aaron was a man of honor. But"—he paused, seemingly trying to sort out how best to explain—"the thing is, war is a different world, and sometimes it makes you do things you wouldn't otherwise do."

Elaine nodded, understanding.

"My unit came across ruined sites sometimes, and sometimes there were valuables left behind. Sometimes...soldiers took things that didn't belong to them," he explained, shame tinging his words. "But," he said, patting his heart a few times with his palm, "I believe that Aaron was just young and naïve, and he was probably worried about having a new baby to support on a first-year army recruit salary."

Elaine stole a glance at Jessica, who was wiping a tear away from her eye.

The room was quiet for what felt like a long time, as everyone reflected on the situation.

Finally Elaine reached out a hand and covered one of Cameron's. "I believe that you were trying to do something you thought would help your family, and I can see that you love your niece and grandniece dearly," she said softly. "But now is the time to make a choice."

Cameron nodded slowly. "I know. I want to do the right thing," he said.

Elaine nodded too, and squeezed his hand before letting it go.

ON THE WAY home from the Lachlans' house, Jan sighed. "I wish I could have done more to comfort Jessica."

Elaine gave her a sympathetic glance before returning her eyes to the road. "I know. She's gone through so much, and none of this was her fault."

"At least Hattie has her bear back," Jan said. "I'm so glad we were able to keep that promise."

"She'll have her tiara back in the morning too. A little less shiny, though, perhaps." Elaine chuckled softly. "Jessica promised to glue a fake gem on instead while Hattie's asleep. And

I gave her the general's address so Cameron can return the diamond to Bruce and his wife."

"So, we are agreed, aren't we, not to say anything to Dan about this right away?"

"Yes," Elaine said firmly as she pulled into the driveway of their home. "We should give Cameron a little bit of time to make things right himself."

"For Cameron's sake, I think that's best," Jan said, unbuckling her seat belt. "And in a few days, we can e-mail General Atkins to find out if his wife's diamond is back in her possession."

CHAPTER EIGHTEEN

The weather was more than cooperative that Saturday before Labor Day—the day of the clambake. A full summer sun shone above as Lancaster locals gathered together to share food, fun, and laughter. Sasha and Brody joined the festivities, as well as all of Jan's family, with the accompanying excitement and shrieks of joy from her grandchildren.

The beach was festooned with Adirondack chairs and long picnic tables covered in blue gingham cloths, and poles stuck into the sand had strands of battery-powered fairy lights strung between them. The scent of clams filled the air. Folks had arrived early to dig a big hole in the beach, which they'd lined with flat rocks. Then the team in charge of the clams had started a fire in the rocks and let it burn out before shoveling away the ashes. Seaweed, brought in from the Maine coast, was layered on top of the hot rocks, followed by lobster, corn, clams, mussels, and potatoes, then topped off with more seaweed and a layer of sand. Everything had cooked up nicely.

Jan and Elaine served iced tea and lemonade until it was time to sit down and enjoy the meal themselves.

"Well, hi there," Jan said, turning to the person seated next to her at the table.

Amber Burgess smiled back at her. "Hi, Mrs. Blake," she said, beaming.

"Are you enjoying your food?" Jan asked, spreading butter on her cob of corn.

"Definitely, but it's not as good as your pastries," Amber said.

Jan smiled. "Which kind was your favorite this summer?" she asked.

"Well, let's see. I liked the chocolate-almond cookies a ton, and the maple croissants, and everything else...but I think the blueberry pie has to be the best," the teenager said with conviction.

As Amber ticked off treats on her fingers, Jan stifled a giggle, then poked Elaine, who sat on her other side, in the ribs, to get her cousin to pay attention. When the young girl finished talking, both women were staring at her with silly grins on their faces.

"What's so funny?" Amber asked, frowning.

"Have you by any chance been leaving reviews of Tea for Two online?" Jan asked.

"Well, yes," Amber said, hanging her head.

Jan and Elaine looked at each other and burst out laughing.

Amber went on. "I had to do some bad ones and some good ones—it was a project for my SAT class, and I was supposed to"—she made air quotes with her fingers—"'demonstrate comprehension' of a certain set of vocabulary words, so I chose to write reviews. I had to use both positive and negative adjectives to describe your food," she said, looking sheepish.

But Elaine and Jan just kept laughing and Amber looked at them like they were nuts.

"Sorry," Amber said, "I promise I'll take them down now that the class is over."

Jan winked. "Only the bad ones, I hope."

AFTER THEY'D FINISHED eating, Elaine left Jan and most of her family playing horseshoes and wandered through the holiday crowd, hoping to run into Jessica. Her thoughts wandered too as she walked, and she was thinking about Sasha when suddenly she heard her daughter's voice from behind.

"Hey, Mom, wait up!" Sasha called. Elaine turned to see her running barefoot through the sand.

"Hi, Sasha, is everything okay?" Elaine asked, wondering why her daughter might have left the family when they were playing one of her favorite games.

"Yeah, actually, everything's great," Sasha said, pulling her brown hair up into a ponytail. Her blue eyes sparkled and there wasn't even a hint of the anxiety Elaine had seen that night when they'd talked about Brody's fear of raising children.

"It's a beautiful day, isn't it?" Elaine asked as they continued through the sand arm in arm, waving at friends as they passed.

"It is," Sasha said, closing her eyes and lifting her chin to let rays of sun soak her face. She opened them and looked over at her mom.

"Do you ever miss Colorado?" Elaine asked.

Sasha studied her feet as they walked, her pink toenails peeking through the sand when she lifted them to take a step. "Full disclosure?" Sasha asked rhetorically. "Sometimes I do. I miss the ski community and some of the friends I made there. And I miss the rugged western history of the state." She smiled at her mom. "It was kind of fun living where pioneers settled all those years ago and started entire cities with nothing more than what they'd brought in their covered wagons. But at the end of the day, I don't miss it enough to need to move back. I think I spent enough time there that a visit now and then will be enough."

"I'm so glad to hear you say that," Elaine said. "I wasn't exactly worried when you talked about what was going on with Brody—I've experienced enough at this stage in life to know that God has a plan for each of us, and it sure seems that Brody could be the one for you. But I worried you might think about escaping back there, and I've gotten really fond of having you here."

Sasha gave Elaine's arm a little squeeze. "I've gotten fond of being here too," she said. "And I get what you mean. I did think about going back, briefly. But that was me trying to run away from what became the first real hurdle for Brody and me to work through, and now I know that staying here and talking it through with him, even though it was hard, was the right thing to do."

"I'm so glad you two were able to overcome that," Elaine said. "The choice of whether to have children isn't easy for everyone, but I had a feeling that with Brody, it was something else holding him back."

"And you were right," Sasha said, nodding her head. "I know you and I haven't had a chance to really catch up since we talked, but when I asked him about it, he said he was worried that, since his parents had so much trouble, that he might not have learned enough about what it means to be a father to take on the role for himself."

Elaine couldn't help the grin that spread over her lips. "That's a very mature thing for a young man to realize," she said.

Sasha returned the grin. "I thought so too," she said.

"What did you say that changed his mind?" Elaine asked.

"Well, we talked about some of the same stuff that you helped me understand—about how no parents are perfect but having each other and a firm foundation with God was a great place to land when things got tough," Sasha said. "And then I told him that, besides the basic provisions, what most kids need to be joyful and at peace is to know that God loves them, and that their parents love them unconditionally. The rest can be messy sometimes, but that's just life."

Elaine stopped walking and pulled her daughter in for a hug, then held her at arm's length. "I'm so glad you two haven't ruled out kids when you get married. I so look forward to meeting them."

Sasha gave her a funny smile. "*When* we get married?"

Elaine blinked, then grinned. "Did I say that? I guess I did!"

Sasha grinned widely this time before giving her mother another quick hug. She looked back up the beach over her shoulder to where the group was still visible, scattered around the horseshoe pit. "I've got to return to the rest of the fam, Mom. Are you coming to join us soon?"

Elaine nodded. "Very soon. I'm just looking for some-one first."

Sasha turned and jogged back the way she'd come, waving as she ran.

At that moment, Elaine turned and spotted Jessica close by, near the water, watching three children play. Hattie was happily using a blue bucket and a small plastic shovel to build a sandcastle with the help of Jan's two little grandsons, Max and Riley. "Look at our castle, Elaine!" Max exclaimed. "Riley did the towers, and Hattie did the moat part."

"Hattie is our new friend," Riley explained, concentrating hard on shaping the castle's turrets.

Hattie nodded in agreement, giving Elaine a shy smile.

"Hi," Jessica said, standing up as Elaine approached. "It's good to see you again."

Elaine smiled, glad to see the young woman looking so much more rested and at ease. Jessica wore a pink tank top over a white knee-length eyelet skirt, and her hair was down around her shoulders, shining in the sun. Her smile carried to her eyes.

"How is your uncle?" Elaine asked.

"He's doing well," she replied. "Things turned out the best they could, given what he did. I still don't know what he was thinking, but I know he was just trying to help Hattie and me. That state trooper—Dan Benson—promised to put in a good word for Uncle Cameron since he returned the jewel to General Atkins. And they were able to match the bullet they found at the break-in to a gun recovered from Tony Lasalle's property, so, with his criminal history on top of all that, he'll be going to prison for a long time."

"Do you think Cameron will have to serve time?" Elaine asked as gently as possible.

Jessica pressed her lips together and looked down at her daughter. "Dan didn't seem to think so. He thinks Uncle Cameron will probably only have to do some community service."

Elaine breathed an internal sigh of relief and sent up a silent prayer of thanks. "What good news!" she said. She bent down to look at Hattie's sandcastle. "That's lovely," she complimented her. "You're a very talented builder."

The little girl beamed.

Max frowned. "Me and Riley are talented builders too," he said, sounding put out.

"I did the towers," Riley reminded Elaine proudly. "And Max made the sand just right—not too wet and not too dry."

"You've all done a great job," Elaine reassured them.

She stood back up, and Jessica was smiling. "Do you want to know what happened to the diamond?" she asked.

Elaine grinned and shaded her eyes with her hand as a sunbeam shot out from behind a cloud. "You know I do."

"Would you believe it?" Jessica chuckled. "The Atkinses gave it to me, of all things," she said.

Elaine's hand flew to her chest, and she was at a loss for words.

"The general and his wife came to see me after Cameron returned the jewel," Jessica explained. "They said they have always been blessed financially, and, even though they never had a child of their own, their lives are filled with nieces and nephews and travel. They said they didn't need any luck the diamond may have brought, and they've lived happily all these years without it." Jessica looked down at her daughter as a single tear slid from her eye. She wiped it quickly away. "The money will be used to pay for Hattie's college when she's older. She can go wherever she wants, and become anything she wants to be."

Elaine felt tears of her own prickling behind her eyes. "That's wonderful," she said, reaching out to grasp Jessica's hand. "I'm so very happy for you and Hattie."

Jessica squeezed Elaine's hand and nodded.

"I hope to see you around town more often," Elaine said. "I hope we can be friends."

A smile spread across Jessica's face, lighting up her eyes. "As far as I'm concerned," she said, "we already are." She gave Elaine a quick hug.

All's well that ends well, Elaine mused as she turned back to rejoin the others gathered around the festivities. She scanned the group that included so many of the people she loved most in all the world, and her heart overflowed with joyous thanks for the bountiful blessings of family and friends God had given her.

ABOUT THE AUTHOR

Amy Woods is the coauthor (with Kristin Eckhardt) of *O Christmas Tea* and author of *A Monumental Mystery* in the Guideposts Tearoom Mysteries series, as well as several other books. She was a reader before she ever dreamed of becoming a writer, and still relishes curling up with a new book by a favorite author more than just about anything else. She and her husband of a decade make their home in Central Texas with their too-smart-for-her-own-good rescue dog.

From the Tea for Two Kitchen

JAN'S FAMOUS LEMON BLUEBERRY SCONES

SCONES:

2 cups all-purpose flour

1 tablespoon baking powder

1/2 teaspoon salt

1/4 cup granulated sugar

6 tablespoons cold
  unsalted butter, cut into
  small pieces

1 cup fresh blueberries

1 tablespoon fresh
  lemon zest

1/2 cup cold heavy cream

1 large egg

1 teaspoon vanilla extract

LEMON GLAZE:

1 cup powdered sugar

2-3 tablespoons fresh
  lemon juice
  (or more to taste)

Preheat oven to 400 degrees. Line a large baking sheet with parchment paper or a silicone baking mat and set aside.

In a large bowl, whisk together the flour, baking powder, salt, and granulated sugar until the ingredients are well mixed. Add the cubed butter and cut it into the flour mixture with a fork or pastry cutter until it resembles coarse crumbs. Add in the blueberries and lemon zest. Gently fold them into the mixture.

In a separate bowl, whisk together the heavy cream, egg, and vanilla extract until fully combined. Pour the mixture into the dry ingredients. Gently fold until just mixed—do not overmix.

Place the dough onto a lightly floured surface and form a ball. Flatten the dough into about a 1-inch-thick circle. Cut the dough into 8 equal sized triangles. Place each triangle onto the baking sheet with a little room between each.

Bake at 400 degrees Fahrenheit for twenty to twenty-five minutes or until they are a light golden brown.

Remove scones from the oven. Allow to cool for at least 10 minutes.

To make the glaze:

Using an electric or hand mixer, blend the powdered sugar and lemon juice until well combined. More lemon juice can be added as needed if the glaze is too thick. If it is too thin, more powdered sugar may be added.

Use a brush to spread the glaze over the top of the scones. Enjoy!

READ ON FOR AN EXCITING SNEAK PEEK
INTO THE NEXT VOLUME OF TEAROOM MYSTERIES!

Turning the Tables
ANNE MARIE RODGERS

O h, look. The house across the street is going up
for sale."

Elaine Cook paused in the midst of dusting a drop-leaf
half-table in the East Parlor of Tea for Two, the Victorian tearoom in central Maine that she co-owned with Jan Blake. The
widowed cousins had purchased the tearoom together a few
years earlier when Elaine had returned to central Maine following her husband's passing. Her short dark hair webbed with
silver, Elaine wore a taupe twinset and matching flats paired
with a forest-green pencil skirt, but she'd tossed a large white
apron over her clothing for the cleaning portion of her day.

Her cousin Jan, conversely, had removed hers because
it had been covered with flour. There also was still a spot of
flour near one temple in her sleek dark hair. Jan already had
been in the kitchen for several hours earlier that morning,
working her baking magic for the day's customers. Dressed in

khakis, comfortable burlap Toms and a tailored white three-quarter-length sleeved blouse, the shorter woman had been kneeling on the chintz cushion of the window seat cleaning the bay windows at the front of the room, but she had paused for a moment, a faded rag and a spray bottle motionless in her hands as she stared out the window.

"The Battie house?" Elaine moved to join Jan at the window and pulled aside one panel of the lace curtain. She narrowed her blue eyes at the bright late-autumn sunshine outside.

Jan nodded. Her eyes, nearly the same blue as her cousin's, glowed with interest. There was an old Victorian across the street from theirs. A woman in a russet suit with a scarf in the shades of an autumn forest knotted at her neck had just finished pounding a "for sale" sign into the leaf-littered grass of the front yard with a rubber mallet. As October wore on, the lawn wore an increasingly thick covering of fallen leaves.

"Hey, isn't that Sharon Reddick?" Sharon was the realtor who had guided them through the process of buying their own home-slash-business.

"Looks like it," Jan said. "She must have gotten the listing."

"I did tell Mrs. Battie what a good job she did for us," Elaine said. Mrs. Battie was the woman who owned the home across the street, though she spent almost all of her time in Florida, and had hardly been in town since they'd opened the tearoom. Still, when they were still looking at the house that would become the tearoom, Mrs. Battie had come over to meet them. When she'd decided to sell the house, she called Elaine from Florida to ask if she had a Realtor recommendation.

When the Realtor returned to the small SUV she had parked at the curb, she put away the mallet she'd been wielding and picked up a sheaf of papers. It took her only a moment to load those into a covered acrylic box attached to the sign.

"I might go grab one of those sets of specs," Jan murmured as the woman climbed into her vehicle and drove off. "I've been curious about that house for ages."

The Victorian was similar to theirs, although it looked somewhat smaller. It belonged to Eleanor Battie, a widow who had spent her entire life in their small town. Sometime before the cousins moved into the neighborhood, Mrs. Battie had decided that she had had enough of Maine winters and moved to Florida just before the first big snow of the season.

Since then, except for a visit or two from Mrs. Battie, the house had stood empty, although routine visits from a landscaping service and a cleaning company indicated that it was being kept up. The cousins and many of the locals who patronized the tearoom frequently wondered if their former neighbor intended to sell it at some point, but no one had known. Until now.

"Oh, look, there's already a notice about an open house." Elaine loved exploring the interiors of homes for sale. Even when she wasn't in the market—which she frequently had been during her husband's years as a career military officer—she still enjoyed viewing layouts and imagining how a home could be improved.

"We should go," Jan said.

"I'm surprised they'd do that right off the bat," Elaine said. "Usually they only host an open house right away if an owner wants a quick sale, or if the Realtor is having trouble moving a house." She pursed her mouth. "Then again, Mrs. Battie may be eager to unload it."

"Speaking of hosting," Jan said, as Elaine let the lace curtain slip back into place and returned to her task, "we need to review our plans for the Autumn Tea."

The cousins had decided to plan a special fall-themed day for the tearoom. They had found that customers, particularly the locals who came in regularly, loved unusual activities. Invariably, the tearoom quickly was booked solid when they announced a special event.

Elaine smiled. "I guess that's coming up soon. I can't believe October's half over." They had planned the Autumn Tea for the latter half of the month. Their special event would feature a quilting bee to complete a harvest themed quilt that would be auctioned off for charity at the annual Chickadee Lake Harvest Home Festival.

"I can't wait for the quilting bee," Elaine said. "Even though I don't quilt, I think it's going to be such fun."

"You still can join us," Jan assured her. "We already have enough experienced quilters signed up. I want to encourage anyone who's interested, even if they don't know how to quilt. We'll have our experienced folks to teach anyone who's new to hand-quilting."

"It almost makes me want to quilt," Elaine said, grinning. "But I'll help Rose and Archie with the tearoom duties that day so that you can focus on the quilting project."

"Camille Lapole called me yesterday to ask how the quilt blocks were coming along," Jan told her cousin. Camille was a friend of Jan's who was a highly experienced quilter. In exchange for a cake for her daughter's upcoming wedding, she had agreed to supervise the quilt project and help with both the morning and afternoon sessions. She had chosen six complementary fabrics, and between her and Jan, they had recruited quilters to piece thirty harvest-themed appliquéd quilt blocks. The quilters could choose to create a design of their own or take a pre-cut package with instructions for a specific block.

"Isn't the deadline for completing the blocks tomorrow?" Elaine asked. When Jan nodded, Elaine said, "And have you received them all?"

"Not all," Jan admitted, "but most of them. I've got a few calls to make."

"Sounds like you're in good shape, though. I ordered the tea we chose yesterday. Have you decided what types of baked goods you want to offer?"

"Tell me about the tea again," Jan said, as she finished washing the final window pane. "Apple something?"

"Harvest Apple," Elaine corrected. "It's a red rooibos made with bits of sweet dried apple, autumn spices, nettle leaf and sunflower petals. It's billed as 'delicious and full-bodied,' according to the Winterwoods Tea Company in Spokane. We've gotten some wonderful products from them before, so I'm confident that this will be tasty."

"It sounds perfect for our autumn celebration," Jan said. "Apples and sunflowers—we can use those as decorating themes, along with pumpkins, gourds, mums, miniature hay bales, and Indian corn." Her eyes sparkled. "I'm excited already."

"What will we serve?" Elaine prompted.

Jan thought for a minute. "How about your mother's pumpkin loaf recipe? It's so beautiful when it's sliced."

"Oh, that's a great idea," Elaine said, thinking of the pretty pinwheel look of the loaf, "and won't Mom be thrilled? We can call it 'Grandma's Pumpkin Roll.'" Her mother, Virginia Willard, had a family recipe that called for a thin layer of pumpkin loaf baked on a jelly roll pan. Turned out onto a clean dish towel well-sprinkled with powdered sugar, the loaf was rerolled in the towel and left to cool while a cream cheese mixture was whipped up, it was then unrolled and spread with the mixture, rolled up again, secured in plastic wrap and refrigerated or frozen. When the cold roll was sliced, the result was a gorgeous spiral effect, and the taste was so sweetly divine few people could eat more than one slice.

"Along with that," Jan said, "I saw a lovely recipe for puff pastry apple blossoms, and for the chocolate-lovers, a chocolate pecan pie."

Elaine pressed a hand to her stomach. "I'm salivating already. And oh, the decorating ideas! I can hardly wait."

"I can hardly wait to see the finished quilt," Jan said. "Those autumn batiks Camille chose are beautiful, and the quilt blocks that have been turned in so far are absolutely stunning. I keep wanting to lay them out and start trying to arrange them, but until we have them all—and until I finish my own—there's no point. We could have it all tentatively arranged and then have to change it if the last one doesn't work in the space left."

Elaine laughed, picking up on the one memorable detail in Jan's words. "The deadline's tomorrow and you're not done with your own?"

"It'll be done before it's needed," Jan said primly, grinning.

"Good morning." A new voice intruded on their merriment. "I've started boiling water since it's nearly time to open. Jan, is there anything special you'd like me to work on today?"

Both cousins turned to greet Rose Young, one of their two employees. The young woman had started as a waitress, but since she'd begun attending culinary school, she had become Jan's invaluable pastry assistant. Her flaxen hair was twisted into a charming up-do this morning, and she already had donned a white chef's coat over her black trousers and blouse.

"Good morning, Rose. I made cream puffs this morning, and I imagine they're cool now. The filling already is made and is in the refrigerator if you want to start with them. We also need to make the ham, brie, and apple crustless sandwiches and whip up some tomato-cheddar on wheat. And just for something different, I made a small selection of spinach and artichoke puff pastries. Recently, we've had several people asking for pastries that are less sweet, so I thought we'd try them."

"Yum. I'll be your taste-tester." Rose grinned, winking one blue eye.

As the pair headed for the kitchen, Elaine walked through the parlors to ensure everything was in place for the day. She filled several sugar bowls and brought fresh napkins up front, so they'd be able to quickly bus and freshen tables.

Then she unlocked the front door, turned over the "Closed" sign to read "Open," and began to sweep off the porch and front steps.

Earl Gray, the resident cat who had adopted them and who lived on their back porch year round—and in a protected shelter during the worst of the winter weather—joined her, his furry tail a stately plume held high above his back as he stalked the broom.

A blue Ford sedan bearing the markings of the Maine State Police pulled to a stop along the curb, and Trooper Dan Benson's tall frame slowly emerged. "'Morning, Elaine." Dan and his family were members of the church she and Jan attended, and since the tearoom had opened, they had worked with him several times in their pursuit of unraveling a mystery. To Dan's exasperation, their methods were not always as straightforward as his, although she rather thought he had grown to respect their abilities.

"Good morning, Dan," she said cheerfully. "Beautiful day, isn't it?"

"It is," he agreed. The sky was clear. Under the morning sun warming the chilly autumn air, Dan's buzz-cut blond hair gleamed as he nodded, confirming his agreement. "Do you think Jan would consider making me a few sandwiches and wrapping up a pastry or two to go this morning? I have to drive over east to Ellsworth to coordinate with another troop's investigation today, and I'm afraid I'm going to get stuck in the car without lunch."

Elaine chuckled, setting aside the broom. "I'm sure she will. Come on in."

Dan followed her into the foyer, carrying his black Stetson uniform hat as he did so. Together they walked back to the kitchen.

"Well, look what the wind blew in," Jan said when she saw him. "Good morning." She had turned on the small kitchen television already, and she reached over and grabbed the remote to lower the volume.

"Good morning." Dan lifted his face slightly and sniffed. "It smells terrific in here. What are you making?"

Jan gave him the rundown of their daily specials. "I know you didn't just stop by to say hello," she added. "What can we get you?"

Dan grinned. "You caught me." He told her what he'd told Elaine about his day's travels. "I was hoping maybe you could make me a couple of sandwiches of whatever you've got. That ham-brie-apple one sounded fantastic. But you don't have to trim the crusts off mine," he added hastily.

Elaine couldn't prevent a snicker. "We wouldn't want your fellow troopers to see you eating sandwiches that didn't look manly." Rose and Jan both laughed, and Dan looked sheepish.

"You said it, I didn't," he pointed out. "But you might be right." They all chuckled again.

"Will you need a drink?" Elaine asked.

Dan shook his head. "I have a supersized insulated mug of coffee in the cruiser."

As Jan's nimble hands began to assemble his sandwiches, Dan said, "So what are you two up to these days? Any new investigations you need help with?"

"Nothing urgent," Elaine told him, gratified that he did indeed appreciate their penchant for solving mysteries.

"We'd be happy to help you out if you have any investigations *you* need help with," Jan told him, turning his offer back on him.

Dan grinned. "We have nothing I can divulge to civilians, but I appreciate the offer."

Jan's cell phone rang then, and she excused herself to answer it. Rose stepped in to finish putting Dan's sandwiches together, while Elaine bagged some of the pastries.

A moment later, Jan stepped back into the kitchen, looking concerned.

"Problem?" Elaine queried.

"Possibly," Jan said. "That was one of the other members of the Chickadee Lake Harvest Home Festival committee. We have to hold an emergency meeting Saturday afternoon. Apparently, the committee chairman, Hester Ronsard, has met with an accident."

"Oh, no. What happened?"

"I don't know," Jan said slowly. "Eulalie didn't have any details. She was just part of a phone tree started by someone else."

"Ronsard," Dan said. "I heard an emergency call go out last night, and I'm pretty sure I heard that name. Does she live near the other end of the lake?"

Jan nodded. "Yes, just outside Penzance."

"I believe someone fell down a flight of stairs," Dan said. "There may have been broken bones and/or a head injury involved. Sorry, I wasn't listening closely. I do know the injured person was transported to the hospital."

"Oh, dear, that doesn't sound good." Jan bit her lip. "The festival is just over two weeks away, and we have a lot of details to finalize."

"I'll add Hester to my prayer list," Elaine said. "I really hope she wasn't badly hurt."

Dan's cell phone rang then, and he pulled it from his pocket. Smiling, he thumbed it on, turned away and said, "Hey, honey, what's up?" Then his body stiffened, and he listened intently. "What? No way…No way! Who told you the police talked to him? Hold on." He turned to the cousins and Rose and said, "Excuse me, please," before disappearing into the foyer at the front of the house.

Elaine frowned. "Sounds like a friend of Dan's must be in trouble."

"Maybe we'd better add Dan to our prayer lists too," Jan said, before they lapsed into an uneasy silence.

Moments later, Dan returned to the kitchen. Rose had finished building his sandwiches, and Jan was bagging them. "Would you please grab a couple of our disposable napkins?" she asked Rose. As Rose entered the pantry, Jan said, "Everything ok?" to Dan.

The trooper shook his head. "Not at all. I just heard that a friend is in some difficulty—" He stopped suddenly, his gaze riveted on the TV.

Following the direction he was looking, Jan quickly turned the volume up so that they could hear. The local news team was breaking a story about a newly discovered theft and potential embezzlement from a statewide nonprofit called Homes for Maine Heroes headquartered in Waterville, just ten miles up the road from Lancaster.

HMH was a stellar organization that built specially modified homes for wounded soldiers and other local heroes like firefighters with polytrauma types of injuries, multiple severe injuries sustained in one event. In some cases, HMH modified an existing home. HMH, the report went on, also provided Maine's heroes with special vehicles and mobility devices to make day-to-day living easier. Unfortunately, the non-profit's Chief Executive Officer, Alex DeRone, had been suspended on suspicion of theft and embezzlement, and charges were pending.

Dan's face had lost all color.

"Dan," Elaine said gently, "is Alex DeRone the friend of whom you were speaking a moment ago?"

Dan nodded. "Yes."

"And you don't believe he's guilty?"

Dan shook his head. "He would never do that."

"You know him well?" Jan asked.

Dan exhaled heavily, his shoulders sagging. "He's been my buddy since I was five years old. We acted as best man in each other's wedding, and we're the godfathers for each other's kids."

Elaine let out a low whistle. "Wow. No wonder you don't believe he would commit a crime."

Dan smiled, but there was no amusement in it. "He wouldn't. Ever. Plus, he loves working for HMH. He would never do anything to harm that organization's reputation. Hearing that funds have been stolen from a non-profit could make donors very leery of giving HMH more money." He shook his head. "Nope. Alex would never do that." He started for the door. "I have to talk to him."

"Dan, wait. Here's your lunch." Elaine grabbed his arm. "Take a deep breath. Maybe you can help get this straightened out, but you can't help him if you're this upset."

"You're right. You're right." He nodded, sucked in a deep breath, and blew it out again. "Thanks." He took the paper bag with his sandwiches and pastries that Jan held out and picked up his hat. "Put this on my tab and I'll catch it later."

"This one's on us," Jan told him, her eyes filled with sympathy. "We'll pray for your friend. Let us know if there's anything we can do."

Dan nodded. "Will do. Thank you." He sounded a little more like himself as he exited the kitchen.

The cousins listened to the trooper's footfalls as he strode across the foyer to the front door and let himself out.

"Well." Elaine shook her head. "I hope he's right about his buddy. He's going to be devastated if Alex DeRone really is the one who embezzled from Homes for Maine's Heroes."

FROM THE
GUIDEPOSTS ARCHIVES

This story, by Judith Hayes of Chatsworth, California,
originally appeared in *Mysterious Ways*

I'd never seen an angrier man. Arms folded, gaze fixed on
the carpet of the hotel ballroom—Earl was by far the most
unpromising participant among the hundred couples who had
come to the marriage-counseling seminar. And I was stuck
with him in my morning breakout group. His face wore a defi-
ant scowl. His wife, Kim, wiped her teary eyes and dabbed at
her cheeks with a tissue.

"I just want us to be happy," she said. "He's always so angry."

Earl unfolded his arms briefly to scratch the stubble on
his chin, but he never looked up at Kim or anyone else. I'd
begun the weekend-long seminar hoping I could help everyone I counseled. And we'd had plenty of successes—most of
the couples were able to start talking, and listening, to each
other again. Others learned that a small act of kindness—like
offering to get their spouses a cup of water or coffee, or even
giving a hug—could start the healing process.

But Earl and Kim? Their marriage seemed doomed. I hurt so much for Kim. Her energy was gentle, loving, soft. Her husband's energy was, well, volcanic.

I tried to draw Earl out with some basic questions about himself and his marriage. "What is this, the Spanish Inquisition?" he shouted, glaring at me.

"See what I mean?" Kim said. "He shouts all the time. He's so defensive. I can't take it anymore."

I was grateful when the morning session came to an end. We wrapped up with a moment of prayer. I closed my eyes and bowed my head. As unpleasant as Earl had been, I prayed for him. *Lord, how can I help someone who is so enraged?*

My eyes remained closed, but something appeared in front of me. The strangest image: a fuzzy brown teddy bear with a plaid bow around its neck. I shook my head to clear my mind.

At lunch, I ate with my husband, Mike, who had sat in on the group and witnessed the whole troubling session. After a few bites I put down my sandwich and leaned close to him. "I know this will sound crazy," I whispered, "but I think I'm supposed to buy Earl a teddy bear."

I explained the vision. How I was out of ideas on how to help this couple. My husband rolled his eyes. "All right. Let's go find a teddy bear."

Fortunately, a store nearby had a large display of teddy bears. I waded through pink teddy bears, white teddy bears and black teddy bears. Some were holding blankets or baby teddy bears or red satin hearts. At last I found a brown bear with fuzzy fur and a plaid bow. Would it help Earl? Or would I end up rescuing it from the trash can?

The seminar resumed and the couples and counselors regrouped. I walked toward the back, where Earl was hiding out, the teddy bear in a brown paper bag under my arm. "Earl? I've got something for you," I said. He barely acknowledged me. I handed him the bag and walked away.

Minutes later, one of the lead counselors stood at the podium at the front of the room and cleared his throat. "Would anyone like to share something they learned in their sessions this morning?" he asked.

Someone stood and moved toward the microphone. The last person I would have expected. He had the bear clutched to his chest; his shoulders were clenched. Was he going to explode?

He said nothing at first. His eyes brimmed with tears. Finally he took a deep breath, composed himself, and began to tell his story. He'd grown up with an abusive father, a man who beat him for every infraction, no matter how slight. Once, as punishment for something, his father grabbed Earl's beloved teddy bear, marched the boy out to the back-yard and threw the bear into the trash incinerator—forcing Earl to watch. My heart ached for Earl—the little boy and the man he'd become.

Earl held up the teddy bear. "God knew I needed this," he said into the microphone. "To remember where my anger comes from. My wife doesn't deserve it. No one does."

He left the podium then, locking eyes with Kim. They met and held each other close, the teddy bear between them.

A NOTE FROM THE EDITORS

We hope you enjoyed Tearoom Mysteries, published by the Books and Inspirational Media Division of Guideposts, a nonprofit organization that touches millions of lives every day through products and services that inspire, encourage, help you grow in your faith, and celebrate God's love.

Thank you for making a difference with your purchase of this book, which helps fund our many outreach programs to military personnel, prisons, hospitals, nursing homes, and educational institutions.

We also create many useful and uplifting online resources. Visit Guideposts.org to read true stories of hope and inspiration, access OurPrayer network, sign up for free newsletters, download free e-books, join our Facebook community, and follow our stimulating blogs.

To learn about other Guideposts publications, including the best-selling devotional *Daily Guideposts*, go to Guideposts.org/Shop, call (800) 932-2145, or write to Guideposts, PO Box 5815, Harlan, Iowa 51593.

Sign up for the
Guideposts Fiction Newsletter
and stay up-to-date on the books you love!

You'll get sneak peeks of new releases, recommendations from other Guideposts readers, and special offers just for you . . .
and it's FREE!

Just go to Guideposts.org/Newsletters today to sign up.

Guideposts.

Visit Guideposts.org/Shop
or call (800) 932-2145

Find more inspiring fiction in these best-loved Guideposts series!

Mysteries of Martha's Vineyard

Come to the shores of this quaint and historic island and dig in to a cozy mystery. When a recent widow inherits a lighthouse just off the coast of Massachusetts, she finds exciting adventures, new friends, and renewed hope.

Tearoom Mysteries

Mix one stately Victorian home, a charming lakeside town in Maine, and two adventurous cousins with a passion for tea and hospitality. Add a large scoop of intriguing mystery and sprinkle generously with faith, family, and friends, and you have the recipe for Tearoom Mysteries.

Sugarcreek Amish Mysteries

Be intrigued by the suspense and joyful "aha!" moments in these delightful stories. Each book in the series brings together two women of vastly different backgrounds and traditions, who realize there's much more to the "simple life" than meets the eye.

Mysteries of Silver Peak

Escape to the historic mining town of Silver Peak, Colorado, and discover how one woman's love of antiques helps her solve mysteries buried deep in the town's checkered past.

Patchwork Mysteries

Discover that life's little mysteries often have a common thread in a series where every novel contains an intriguing whodunit centered around a quilt located in a beautiful New England town.

To learn more about these books, visit Guideposts.org/Shop